EVA'S STORY

EVA'S STORY

Linda D. Cirino

Ontario Review Press, Princeton, NJ

The Ontario Review Press
9 Honey Brook Dr.
Princeton, NJ 08540

Distributed by W. W. Norton & Co., Inc.
500 Fifth Avenue
New York, NY 10110

Library of Congress Cataloging-in-Publication Data

Cirino, Linda D.
   Eva's story / Linda D. Cirino — 1st ed.
      p.   cm.
   Originally published: The egg woman. 1997.
   ISBN 0-86538-097-X (pbk. : alk. paper)
   1. World War, 1939–1945—Germany Fiction. 2. Holocaust, Jewish
   (1939–1945) Fiction.   I. Title.
   PS3553.I748E92   1999
   813' .54—dc21   99-24388
                                                        CIP

First Edition

EVA'S STORY

Southwestern Germany, 1936

ONE

I come from a long line of farmers. And farmers' wives. There is a picture of a woman farmer on the sack of corn feed we use that shows the woman just the way I've always seen most farmers, looking down. I don't know what she's supposed to be doing on the bag of feed, but she could be bending her head to some work in the house or in the field, some mending or cooking, tending the children. Every once in a while, just to check the weather, I'll take a look at the sky, see how the setting sun tells the next day's temperature, see if storm clouds will come over before the laundry is dry. Mostly, though, my head is bent over, like hers. As far back as anyone can recollect, we have been working the land.

Our farm is small, small enough for the two of us to manage and small enough so that we have nothing much left after the full accounting is made. We are not among the large landholders and substantial farmers. We do not rent out our far pasture for some poor family to plow. We do not hire people to help us bring in the wheat when it's ready. When we were really busy we used to have the children stay home from school to help us out. We grow most of our own food for the table, but we don't have much left over to sell at market. Well, during the summer months, we can bring a few tomatoes and greens, and some extra potatoes and onions now and then, but it would be too much trouble to expand our small vegetable garden for the little additional income it might bring in. There are some large farms in this area I'm told, but ours is not one of them.

When you approach our farm from a distance, if you are new to this part of the world, you would see nothing to differentiate it from others around here. You see our small house, the barn off to the left and the barnyard extending in front and to the left of it until it's bounded by the chicken coop. The house has some straggly flowers in front by the steps and the vegetable garden at the back. When you get closer, you can see the house is small, only four rooms, not counting the cold room. Upstairs are the two bedrooms, each just about big enough for the beds, and downstairs, the kitchen, the front room, and the cold room off the kitchen where we store things. The steps leading to the front door turn into a short porch before you can pull the bell. Most times strangers pull too hard on the bell and scare themselves, me and the chickens. But we need the bell to be loud, because it isn't really a doorbell as such, but a lunch and dinner bell and for emergencies. The house is just big enough for us; there is enough space in each room for what we have. The house is similar to the one I grew up in, so it has always felt right to me.

The presence of the animals makes itself felt as soon as you get near the fence. The fence goes along the road and delineates the yard near the barn. Within the fenced area the animals can mingle, but they don't. You see the cows linger near the gate, and the pigs hunkering down in the shade, and the chickens chasing each other in the enclosure just in front of the coop. You will probably smell the cows before you get too close and once you do it will be some time before you get used to it. Eventually, like me, it won't bother you any more, but at first I know it's a bit pungent. The cows don't make as much noise as the chickens will if you get up close; they will set up a squawking and take refuge in the coop if they think you want to look at them. After a short while the noise and smell will subside on their own and you will be struck by how disorganized everything seems. We have so much to do that we have never been able to do the extra things that might make the place neater and more orderly. So we have more messes in the yard than we would like and we have to step carefully, just like you would if you go in the animal area.

The vegetable garden is overrun with weeds and unruly plants, some wildflowers plant themselves in between the lettuce and beets making it look a bit confused. We can't really concentrate on just the vegetables when we have to worry about the rest of the farm. My husband keeps himself busy with the wheat and corn in the field across the road. I have to tend the house, the garden and the animals. He brings me the water for the day before he leaves in the morning and tells me what needs doing. I ring for him at lunchtime and he does what I can't do for me. Then he goes to his job at the stone works and sometimes delivers some eggs in the village on his way. He comes back for dinner and asks me if everything went okay for the day and sees to anything that needs it.

I keep the books for the farm, because my husband never went further than the early years of school. My family was large, so they did not mind me staying in school until I got married. I wasn't needed so much at home and my brothers were able to do what needed doing. So I am able to do some adding and record keeping, even though my husband looks over my shoulder and worries me the whole time. I don't say he can't read at all, and he can write his name nicely, but it isn't an everyday thing to do. As I think about it, I doubt he ever read a proper book, I mean a grown-up book, from cover to cover. I liked to read stories to my children at bedtime and he listened along with them. I know he did, because sometimes when I would stop before the end, because maybe they had fallen asleep or the story was too long and my throat was sore, he would ask me how it turned out. As I said, our house is small, and he could hear me well enough if he were lying in our bed in the next room, or sitting by the stove downstairs. I had hoped the children would keep their schooling as long as they could. They grumbled every time I told them that, but I thought that they might have need of it when they got married, like I did.

My children's growing up followed a different pattern from my own. They were part of an adventure that they dedicated themselves to with enthusiasm and a sense of excitement. The success of the enterprise, so they were convinced, depended on their total and constant commitment and obedience which they gave with a sense of abandon and, indeed, joy. They were so involved in their participation that small personal matters lost significance, down to disappearing altogether. We older people were the opposite. To us there was nothing of importance beyond the farm itself and surviving from one harvest to the next. To this we had dedicated ourselves, and all the rest was distraction.

From a distance you might think the farm is peaceful and restful, but that is just because it lies nicely in its space. A soft rise behind the vegetable garden cushions the house and a large meadow extends behind the barn. The buildings—the house and the barn and the coop—blend into the trees and hills around it. The farm looks right as it sits there. You think it belongs there, and it does. The ones that had it before us were there for a hundred years or so, chipping away at the land until there was left just the amount we have. They would have stayed, farming still, if they hadn't been hit by the fever. They all had it and finally had to sell this farm to us. We were young then and the farm seemed so large and full of hope and future wonders. Now we know that the hope was just to get us through each season and the future wonders did not exist.

I was sixteen when we came to live here. I know numbers well enough to know that it was more than half a life ago for me. Now I'm about halfway through my whole life, I guess. The house looked bigger when we first came here to live. I had never done so much cleaning and fixing as then. It seemed I had not enough time to do everything for just the two of us. Now, after the two children have begun their own lives, I manage just fine—better than I did then, at least. I was overwhelmed. I had seen my husband from a distance only when he came to ask my father if he could marry me. I knew where he lived and my father asked around and heard he was a good worker and not violent. This proved to be true. My father came to me and told me it was my time and he had spoken to this person and he could take care of me and keep me in a good life. My father said he had brought me up so far and now it would be Hans's duty to provide for me. It would be my duty to be a wife and if I did all the wifely things, I would be provided for and safe for the rest of my life. My father was pleased that he could see me settled and started on a family the way it should be. He told my husband that he couldn't give me much in the way of dowry, but that he would do what he could each year on my birthday. My husband agreed to this, because my father had a reputation as a decent man and because he saw that I was strong and able to help him. He knew I had had some schooling and so he thought I would have a strength where he had a weakness. In our bedtime matters, it turned out he knew as little as I, despite the fact that he had had four more years to find out about it. His interest in bedtime things was sporadic and only for the first year or so did he think about my pleasure. He seemed to forget after a while. During that first year he would sometimes come home before I rang the lunch bell and he would find me in the vegetable garden and we would lie down between the rows and he would unfasten my apron and lift up my skirt. If he caressed me slowly, if he kissed my neck, I would look up at the sky and rock with him until he was spent and then I would feel the pleasure.

After the baby came there was no more chance for pleasures in the vegetable garden. I never refused his overtures and never made any of my own. The baby took one's mind off such things. I liked the baby even though it seemed to be up to me to do for it until he would be old enough to help with the chores. I preferred tending to the baby to some of the other things I was responsible for, but those things still needed doing too.

My husband milked the cows in the morning, before breakfast. He fed the horses, pigs and chicks and gathered the eggs. Then he went to the field. I tended the vegetable garden and the house, I did the laundry and cooking, and after lunch when my husband went to work, I tended to the animals and the baby and whatever else needed doing. It was not difficult so much as it was constant. There is never really a moment of repose. After the first baby came,

I was soon pregnant with the second, and until they went off to school I had my hands full.

I can't complain about my husband. He works hard and long. When we decided to come to the farm, he knew we wouldn't be able to live off it. More or less the farm is my lookout, except that he gives it the mornings. If I weren't here to keep things going on the farm, he wouldn't be able to manage alone. He would have to move into town and work at the stone works full-time. We both are used to farm life, so this arrangement is preferable.

To look at my husband tells you a lot about what it is like to live with him. His face is long and thin with lines cutting into his cheeks from his cheekbones to his chin. His eyes are clear blue, his hair a dark brown layer covered by a lighter blonder layer on top. His hair is straight and long; I cut it for him when it begins to fall too far into his eyes. His hair is thick but fine and he has always worn it just this way, with the part just off the center to the left. He laughs very rarely. Sometimes the children used to amuse him. More often he keeps his mouth tight and straight, neither bending up or down. It's like there is no expression at all in his face. I can tell if he is displeased or annoyed or tired, but my father was a good judge of him and he has never been angry or aggressive toward me. Neither has he ever been loving or affectionate. The pleasuring we have shared is not a sign of feeling but of physical need. Life between my husband and me, I would say, is busy. There is not too much time to dwell on feelings, even if there were any. My husband and I follow a tradition of farming folk who know no other way. Each day duplicates the previous one depending only on the changing of the seasons. There is a certain comfort in the repetition of daily routines. On a farm one knows that one is needed for the growing of the animals and wheat. If we were not here on the farm, there would be no one to continue it.

Although there is a trend now to city life, we know very little about it. Over the years since we came here many of the neighbors have up and left, given up farming altogether. Who can say how it is?

We had no way of knowing what life is like in towns and cities. My husband sometimes carried home stories from someone at the stone works who had been there, but we never put much stock in those tales. Once my husband told me about a square in the center of a city that they say could hold thousands of people at a time and that someone had seen it. My husband didn't argue with this man, but when he told me about it, he said he didn't believe it. He said it was pure exaggeration.

My experience was limited to farm work. I did not imagine that others could busy themselves in the city with no animals and fields to tend to. I felt that were I to find myself suddenly transported to a city, I would be as useless as a baby, unable to provide for myself even the basic necessities of food and clothing. To me, in my imagination, everything in the city would be done differently, one would need to learn a completely new usage for each moment of the day.

The time I'm speaking about was a time when things around us were changing. Many of these changes we were too busy to be aware of. They didn't really concern us all that much. We were married after the Great War and we moved to the farm we still are living on. At first it seemed we might be able to make it with the farm only, but when times got bad for us they were getting bad for everyone. The prices for wheat and potatoes were way down and when my husband went to look for work to supplement the farm income, he couldn't find anything. After one or two bad years, so bad that we had to ask my father for an additional portion to get us through, things began to even out again and my husband found this job with the stone works that, even if it is only half-time, still helped us pull even.

One afternoon when my husband was at his job, the government Food Bureau man came by and made an inspection tour around the farm, writing down everything he saw. He said we might be eligible for some benefits, like loans or reduced prices for feed. My husband had heard about this already from talk in the village. To get these new benefits we had to show our birth certificates and those of our parents. This we did and we eventually got our feed at cheaper prices and if we needed a loan we were able to get one. From then on this government man made regular visits to the farm, usually in the afternoon, and wrote down in his book any changes, like if there were baby pigs, how many bushels of potatoes we had harvested, things like that. Sometimes he suggested that we do something different and I would tell my husband. Usually it wasn't a big thing and we might or might not do it.

Of course, the biggest change for us was when my husband was called to the army. One day when he came back from the stone works he told me that all the men were being called into the army. Although we had very little money put aside, my husband told me that he would offer the government man something to declare our farm necessary for war preparations. This would mean that my husband would not have to go into the army, but could stay and farm. The government man took the money my husband offered him and said he would see what he could do. I guess it wasn't enough, because my husband had to report to the army and we never got the money back.

When my husband left he told me how he wanted me to run everything while he was gone. He said I would be able to make a go of it by myself. Of course, the children had to help too. He told me to concentrate on two places, the vegetable garden, mainly for our own food, and the chickens. He calculated that the chickens would be our source of take-in from the outside. We would increase the flock and I would bring the eggs to the village every other day and sell them, giving us enough money to carry on. Before he left, my husband expanded the chicken coop a bit and replaced some rotting boards and enclosed an area in front of it to separate the chickens from the other animals. My husband described how to do for the chickens and where to take the eggs.

My husband was right that we could manage ourselves. Not everything was as he planned, but we managed. The first problem I faced was the children. The farm depended on their energies to operate smoothly. When my husband left he assigned each one to do certain chores. The girl was to milk the cows in the afternoon and see to the large animals. The boy was to keep the tools in good order and keep the fields in shape. He had to bring in the water every day before school and keep up with repairs. It didn't always work out this way. It seemed that the children were spending less and less time at home. I asked the boy why he came home so late and he said, "The Youth had a meeting."

"How come," I wondered, "you don't tell your Youth leader that you must go home to help on the farm?"

He said, "The Youth is more important than the farm. I told them once or twice I needed to come home and they punished me for missing meetings."

"Maybe you should withdraw from the Youth," I suggested. "Your father is in the army. Isn't it sufficient for one man in the family to be doing patriotic work? Especially since we need your help."

"But everyone is in the same situation. If they punish me more times, they will doubt my commitment and eventually they will expel me. If they expel me, I will be labeled a troublemaker and no one will dare buy our eggs any more."

I said nothing further and my son continued to spend more time with the Youth. The field became more or less a shambles. When the government man came by, he saw the field was in disarray and he asked about it and made some notes in his book.

The girl likewise began to spend more time at the Girls' League. I found myself more and more overwhelmed with chores. Now I had to milk the cows morning and evening, see to the garden, do the cooking and laundry and house upkeep and tend the chickens. Every other morning I went into the village and delivered the eggs.

When the government man told me I would have to sell the horses, I knew he was right. We could no longer maintain the horses, feed them and otherwise see they were healthy since we were using them for fieldwork so rarely. Actually when he mentioned it my first reaction was to thank him, because I saw this solution as a relief. When I returned from the village, I would be struck by the state of the fields and other, more pressing, chores to be done.

We sold the horses. The government man handled it for me. I had no idea how to go about such a business. I did not know who to sell to or how much I should get. With the money, we were able to pay for some new material for clothing and some better feed for the chicks.

When my husband left in June we had about twenty-five layers and four cocks in the coop. We had discussed with the government man our plans to increase the flock to about one hundred. We were to receive larger supplies of feed and our monthly quota would grow according to our progress. The first step was to sell only the oldest birds and only those that were obviously freakish. The remainder would be left to provide as many chicks in the new year as we could get. For the last six months of the year, we would keep as many birds as we had, even if they weren't laying. This was our initial investment in enlarging the egg business. The extra feed required to carry over these birds came in part from our own wheat harvest. There was abundant wheat that year as my husband had planted an extra patch.

Just after we sold the horses my husband came home on leave. He understood about the horses and spent most of the two weeks bringing in the wheat from the field. He had been granted his leave at this time specially to help with the harvest. He was pleased that the eggs were providing us with some income and would meet our needs as the flock grew. One afternoon, my husband was working in the field and I went to the chicken coop to gather the afternoon eggs. I began to hum the little tune that the chickens like to hear, so that they know it's me. I always hum the same tune, it seems to calm the birds down a bit and prepare them for my opening the door. This time when I opened the door someone grabbed me from behind and put his hand over my mouth and whispered in my ear, "Please don't yell, I won't hurt you. Please let me stay. My life is in danger. Please don't give me away or I will be killed." I tried to see who was holding me, but he had grabbed my arms and was directly behind me whispering in my ear. My heart was a-gallop, but his voice was soothing and frightened. I sensed immediately he wouldn't hurt me, but was himself in peril. He turned me toward him so that I could see him, releasing my mouth but signaling me not to say anything or call out, begging me with his eyes not to give him away. As soon as I saw his face, I relaxed. This was no criminal, this was a person who was himself completely terrified, not intending to attack me. I said nothing, but as I looked at his eyes my body relaxed. He looked at himself to see what I was seeing that so relaxed me and began brushing at the bits of straw and sawdust that covered his clothes. He explained where he came from in a hoarse whisper, as I stood there unable to speak or move. "I escaped. I am a student from the university. I was put in the camp because I refused to leave the university. I escaped. Please let me stay here. I won't hurt you. Please don't give me away. I will be killed on the spot if you do." Still I said nothing and didn't move, but my mind was racing. There was no moment when I thought to give him away. I was not at all frightened of him or that he was there. I knew my husband was across the road, but I didn't need reassurance for I felt no fear. I knew what to do and would do it. I acted decisively as though finding runaways on the farm was a weekly event. I went to the nook under the roost and motioned him to follow me. He ducked under the shelf and found a spot out of the light, where he crouched down, and as I was turning to leave he grabbed my hand and looked in my eyes with gratitude. He had no need to say anything, I saw in his eyes what he felt. I gathered the eggs and left the coop.

As I left the coop, I was more agitated than I realized. My body was trembling, my heart and blood racing, and my eyes searching for signs that there were visitors elsewhere on the farm. Perhaps, I thought, there are others somewhere, in the barn, in the house. Maybe my husband has been accosted by someone as I had been. I saw nothing that indicated anyone else was on the farm, or that the man in the coop had been observed.

In the time it took me to put the eggs in the cold room, I was able to get my body quiet and my face back to usual. I had no thoughts then about telling or not telling my husband; I was just trying to recover from the several shocks—the surprise, the first moment of fear, my having tacitly accepted this person to hide in the coop. I wasn't yet sure he was also to be hiding from my husband. Just as I was quieting myself and sorting out the eggs, my husband came into the house and began discussing with me about the field and how our boy could be doing something to help bring in the wheat. As I think back now, I see that it was then, that moment, that I should have told my husband about the person in the coop. After all, such an unusual thing happens, I should have told him, interrupted what he was saying to tell him someone had accosted me in the chicken coop and was hiding under the roost. But I wasn't ready to tell my husband. I didn't know in that very instant that there would never be a fit moment. The secret was created in that moment, unpremeditated, guilelessly. The secret grew from those first thoughtless, intuitive occasions when I might have, but didn't, tell my husband. I was not thinking in terms of protecting the man; I didn't particularly feel I was hiding him, but that he was there. I did not understand the danger he spoke about, but there was that look in his eyes when I left that told me I would not reveal his presence. It was that one instant, his reaching out for my hand and looking at me so intensely, a look that reminded me of a dog we once had who cowered and peeked at us from the corner of his eyes, acknowledging his vulnerability, but challenging us to find the grace to forgo such easily accomplished hurt. He gave me with this look, a straight look, directly in my eyes, his so dark, a trust and a promise. The trust was his confidence that I would not betray him, that I would not give his whereabouts away, the promise was that he would never forget that he owed me this particular moment of his existence.

As I sorted the eggs, gently tapping one against the other to check for cracks in the shells, and later, half-listening to my husband's description of how to tend the field, I thought about what had taken place in the chicken coop. I did not know why the man had come to be there, but I understood that something had taken place between us. I was protecting this man now, even from my husband.

From that moment the man in the coop was in my thoughts. When the children returned home and took up the chores, as I prepared our dinner, as we put the kitchen in order afterwards, I thought about the moment I would go to change the water and lay out feed for the chicks. I like to postpone this feeding as long as possible, so that the chickens have a nice amount of feed when they wake up, so I won't hear their complaining first thing in the morning. As I was going through the usual routine, I was preoccupied with the thought of seeing this man again in the chicken coop. I had surreptitiously put some bread and a potato from our dinner into my apron pocket, rather than keeping it over. We often gave the chickens scraps from the leavings on our plates and the fixings from cooking. This time I brought with me fresh water, fresh corn and wheat and what I had in my pocket. As I walked across the barnyard to the chicken coop, I began to hum my usual tune and made a particular effort to slow my step. My husband was fixing a tool in front of the barn and as I opened the door to the coop, I knew that he would be able to see what I did. I opened the door and stepped in, still humming, and put the water pail down just inside. Before picking up the trough to toss out the stale water, I tossed behind me the bread and potato, into the darkness under the roost, I still humming. I threw the water out the door, glancing over to where my husband was still working, and went back in the coop. I put in the fresh water, the grain, and checked over the chickens quickly, looking about the coop. I saw that he was already eating the food, crouched quite far under the roost, watching me. I closed the door and left.

As I lay in bed, my husband now by my side, I was glad I had given the stranger the bread and potato. I wondered what he had meant about escaping and the camp and being killed. I thought of asking my husband, who would know these things, but I could think of no way to raise the subject without revealing the man's presence in the chicken coop. My husband was due to return to the army in three days' time, but I wasn't concerned about him finding the man. I wasn't thinking about keeping the man there for three days undetected. I was wondering would he be there in the morning when I went to feed the chicks.

Over the next three days I followed the same routine. I tried to add something to the meals I prepared, figuring on bringing a portion to the man in the coop. My husband did not seem to notice anything different, his thoughts were on his return to duty and what that would bring for him. He did not indicate that he considered how his departure might affect me, other than my need to maintain the farm and ourselves, mainly by selling the eggs. I wouldn't say he said much of anything anyway, except for giving instructions to me and the children. Aware that he would soon be leaving, we didn't object or complain, knowing we would soon be on our own again. There was a moment just before my husband left when I thought he might be about to tell us he would miss us, but I could see that he was preoccupied with his own survival and we didn't really feature in his thoughts much.

Each of us was concerned with our own dilemma. He mentioned the war talk that circulated around the army post, next to which selling eggs must have seemed a triviality. I was apprehensive that I might fail to succeed with the egg project and have to give up the farm. My husband and I both regarded such an eventuality as a disastrous end to our years of work on the farm. It was to be up to me to prevent losing the farm and I wasn't convinced I could do it.

It was a Sunday when he left and the children were home and we stood there in the road as he walked toward the village, just like any family would. When he reached the bend in the road, he turned around and waved and we were still standing there, waiting for just this, and we waved back. He could see the house and the barn and the barnyard with the field across the road, all of it, including the two children and myself, at our best, without the details that showed how things really were. We looked like a picture-book scene, but we didn't feel that way. I was thinking more about the man hiding in the coop than the man down the road leaving for the army.

When the children left for school the next day, I went directly to the chicken coop, automatically humming to calm the chickens. I had already fed and watered the birds and gathered the morning eggs, but I had the first chance since he had come to talk to the man in the coop. As I approached and opened the door, the man was not under the roost, but standing near the doorway. Having seen the children leave that morning and my husband the day before, he knew that there were no others about the farm. He greeted me by hugging me to himself, saying "thank you" over and over. I was again shocked at his touch, not being in the habit of hugging. I pulled myself separate and took another look at the man, really for the first time since the first day. His greeting had put me off balance. I lowered the window covers to calm the birds so that we might talk for a few moments without overexciting the chickens.

His clothes were all brown, with mud patches here and there, pants and shirt the same nondescript color. The cuffs and pockets of both trousers and shirt were torn unevenly, in some places frayed from a rip. The trousers hung low on his hips as though a size or two too large and the legs were dragging through the litter on the floor of the coop. His face had a sweet expression, his lips in a half-smile. His eyes and eyebrows reacted energetically to his words. He had a half-inch growth of beard, black like his unruly longish hair. He wore a tipsy pair of glasses, lacking an ear-piece and one lens cracked, but evidently essential. His raggedy appearance did not disguise a natural grace. He spoke quietly and calmly, but with great intensity.

"Thank you for bringing me the food, ma'am. I am most obliged for such kindness. I drank some of the chicken water. I hope it was allowed. Thank you for saving my life, ma'am."

"Why is your life in jeopardy, young man?" I asked. "What did you escape from in the first place? What have you done?"

"I've done nothing at all. I was told to leave the university because I couldn't produce the proper papers. I refused to leave. I must finish my studies. I was arrested and put in a camp in Mauernich and I escaped."

"Mauernich? Where is that?"

"About three days' walk from here toward the east."

"How long were you to be at this camp?" I asked.

"I don't know. I had been there something over a month. I think it was just a holding place. They wanted to send me away, out of the country," he said.

"Just for not having the right papers?" I asked.

"That's what it amounts to, ma'am," he answered.

"What do you plan to do?" I asked him.

"I don't really have a plan, ma'am. I hoped you would let me stay here awhile," he answered.

"A few more days will be no problem." I answered rather abruptly, raising the window covers, bewildered both by what he said and the feeling of something that remained unsaid.

As I returned to the house, I knew there would be no such thing as a few more days. I did not yet fully understand why he had been arrested and sent to the camp. He had answered all my questions, but nonetheless I had no idea what he had done. I had no further idea of what to ask, even though he was apparently perfectly ready to answer my questions, and, it seemed, honestly. I needed time to think these fragments of information over to see what they might mean and what else I might ask. As it was we had spoken together longer than I was used to talking with anyone. I had no background for interrogating him.

That evening when I brought his food, I brought him a bucket for his needs, beginning a new routine of collecting the bucket each morning on my way to the outhouse with the bucket we used for the same purpose overnight in the house.

We continued this way for a week longer. Then my children were scheduled to go with their Youth groups to a retreat to the mountains. The boy had packed his gear and set off on Friday afternoon after school to join his group. He had received permission from his father to participate in this hiking expedition with his club. The girl likewise had pressed her uniform and bandanna and packed her things, including her needlework project, and headed off for a weekend of workshops and home studies. When I was alone on the farm, except for the man, I went to the coop as usual after the evening meal with water and feed for the chicks and something for him. This time I brought a complete plate of food, since there was no one to observe. As I tended the chickens, I heard him eating and scraping the food from the plate quite hungrily. I had been so complacent in thinking that the little bread and food I brought could be sufficient for a man his size and youth. Of course, I had nowhere near approached the amount that would satisfy his hunger. I had imagined that the token food I had thought so significant, having been taken in stealth and tossed to him under the roost as to a dog, could satisfy his hunger. Inwardly I cursed myself for having been such a fool and from then on I brought him an equal portion to what we had. I managed to bring him something in the morning and at noontime, until I judged he had enough to keep him from being so hungry.

The next day, Saturday, I suggested when I arrived in the morning that he might like to come out to the house for a change. He immediately agreed and followed me, cautiously, across the barnyard to the house. He sat in the kitchen as I collected the things I needed to take to town. Saturday, of course, was market day, and as a rule I took a larger basket of eggs and a few chickens with me to the village market. He watched me assemble my things, the eggs slung in a basket over my shoulder, the two chickens in one hand flapping a bit, and in the other a sack of potatoes and onions. I would make a nice bit of change this day, enough for a new ration of feed and maybe some meat.

"I think you can stay here until I come back this afternoon," I told him. I imagined it must be a bit trying spending each day crouched under the roost in the company of the chickens. So I let him stay in the house.

When I walked into the house in the early afternoon, I saw the downstairs rooms were empty and as I went up the stairs I could see through the doorway that he was stretched out on my bed. The noise of my shoes on the bare steps woke him and as I came in the room he sat up on the side of the bed. "I hope you don't mind, but it had been so long since I could stretch my legs out and since I had a soft bed to sleep on, not that the chicken house is not good enough, it's more than good enough for me and I appreciate your letting me use it, but this bed brings back memories and I couldn't resist. I hope I haven't offended you by sleeping on your bed."

"No." Seeing him sitting on the edge of the bed, the only other person who had ever been in this room, except for myself and my husband, and the children, of course, surprised me. I did not feel offended at his using the bed, so much as stunned that such a thing had taken place. It was as if, looking in the mirror as I fastened my hair, I were to see a new face. It was totally unexpected and rather eerie. I had not clearly grasped how it was to live in the chicken coop. I saw that my reaction had inspired his apologetic explanation, but in fact I was just surprised. "I had quite a successful day at the market and I came back empty-handed, but not empty-pocketed," I said.

"I'm glad for you," he said. "Was the market crowded today? What do they talk about in the village these days?"

"I don't talk with the villagers, I just sell my wares."

"Oh, I see."

"Do you want some supper?"

"Thank you, yes."

And he followed me down the stairs to the kitchen. Hearing his steps behind me, in the house, the new tread reminded me that it was only he and I who knew that we were alone in the house. There had never before been an occasion on which I departed from the usual farm routine. I did not consider there was anything improper, but just something no one would have guessed about. My husband would never have conceived I would be in our kitchen with a strange young man preparing a meal for us. My children probably could not imagine anyone in our home but ourselves. There was a novelty about his presence in the kitchen. I put a few things together for the meal, gathered some things for the soup and set it to cook on the stove. All the while he watched me as he sat at the table. I didn't feel he was much in a hurry to eat, he was just enjoying the scene of my preparing the food. He never took his eyes from my hands.

As we sat across from each other at the table, eating our meal, he must have realized the uniqueness of the occasion. For him, certainly, to eat at a table, like a member of the family, in the warm kitchen, with no chickens pecking around, must have been most enjoyable. For me, of course, I looked up and rather than my husband, I saw this young person, with such dark eyes and thick curly dark brown-black hair. As we ate, from time to time I would look up and be shocked not to find my husband. My eyes forgot each time I raised them, though I myself did not forget for a moment who it was I was sharing this meal with. The silence between us was a totally different sort of silence from that which hung over the table when my husband and I shared a meal. This time the silence was more a quietness, a pause. I did not so much glance up at him as I raised my eyes and looked at him, watched him eat, until he felt my eyes on him and he looked at me and I lowered mine, not quickly, but from shyness. I did feel a certain shyness, embarrassment; the newness of the situation was a little hard for me to get used to. Once our eyes connected across the table, he already watching me and me looking up from my soup and not feeling so shy, but keeping my eyes up and continuing to look at him.

When we finished eating he brought his plate to the sink and some of the other items from the table. He saw that I needed extra water, which I had failed to replenish that morning, and he took the bucket and went to the well, where he had seen us all fill up the bucket. I took the water he brought and used it to finish washing the dishes, he standing by and watching.

When it came time to go out to the chicken coop to feed and water the chickens, he asked if he could carry the pail and I let him. We went to the coop and did for the chickens. When we had finished, I felt it would be awkward for him to sleep in the chicken coop, when he could as well stay at the house. "The children are not coming home tonight, perhaps you would like to stay in the house for a change."

"I would like that very much," he said.

So he came back to the house with me from the chicken coop and spent the night there. I took out some mending work and my sewing case and sat in my usual chair, repairing some clothes. He sat in the other chair, where my husband used to sit, and watched me. I kept feeling that he wanted to say something. But I had no habit of chitchat and I had nothing to say, so we just sat like that, not talking at all. This time, there was an awkwardness in the room. Finally, I became so uncomfortable with the feeling that he wanted to say something that I asked him, "Did you want to say something?"

"Many things. But I don't know which of them to say."

I did not know how to respond to that. I had invited him to say whatever he wanted, and he ended up saying nothing.

A little while later, embarrassment still heavy in the room, he began. "I want to thank you for your goodness toward me. I have had so much time to think. Not only in this last week, but for the last year and more. I have felt like the fountain in the square, that people know, see every day, pay no real attention to. I have felt that people do not care what I feel. At the university, first they ignored me. My professors refused to call on me and when I made appointments to discuss my work with them, they refused to see me. They failed me in all my courses. My fellow students likewise ignored me. They brushed by me, pushed me out of the aisles, bumped into me so that my books scattered in the mud, spilled ink on my papers. These students were like those who see a fountain in the square and decide it stands for something they don't like. Instead of ignoring it only, they have to chip away at it, mar it, make their mark on it in order to take a stand against it and disassociate themselves from it. They can't do this under cover of darkness, they must show the world that they do not like this fountain and what it stands for. They do not think, I don't like this fountain, but let it be, someone will like it. That would not be enough to their credit. They can only distinguish themselves from the fountain by defiling it in public. For this reason I am more than grateful for your kindness to me. How can I really thank you?"

"There is no need. You have."

"You have accepted me here with such ease, perhaps you do not realize the fate that awaits me. I feel that you welcome me without wondering who I am really, what I am."

Well, I knew he was no criminal, he told me that he was a student the first day he came. He looked like a student— I mean, there was something about him that didn't look like a farmer. I did wonder why he had trouble at the university, but I did not have the courage to ask. I felt that if I asked a particular question he might feel his answer would determine if I allowed him to remain. On the contrary, however, I had no thought of asking him to leave. I did not want to ask him something merely to satisfy my curiosity. He no doubt thought that what he had told me was sufficient for me to understand, but I did not. Mainly I wondered how long he expected to stay in the chicken coop. Partly for fear that he would consider it a request to leave, partly, I think, for fear that he would leave, I preferred not to ask. So I did not say anything.

As I lay on my bed, later that night, I had difficulty falling asleep, my thoughts turning to him lying in the next room in the boy's bed. I resisted the urge I felt to peek into the room to see how he looked while he slept, since the squeak of the floorboards might wake him up. But his presence was felt in the house.

The next day, Sunday, there was much to do, especially without the children around to help. I had to do those of their chores that could not be deferred and my usual farm-day routines. He came down to have some coffee shortly after I did, probably having heard the inevitable noise made by the slightest movement in the house, and asked me if he could do something for me. I let him do some weeding in the garden and I gathered the eggs, tended the chickens and did the other chores. As I was slopping the pigs and cleaning the barn where it needed it, I heard him approach from behind. He pulled the barn door to halfway and came toward me. He took my hand and led me to a place where the clean straw was piled and sat me on it. In the dimness he held my hand. He put his arm around my shoulders, still holding my hand in his. I thought he would be telling me something, like maybe goodbye, so I waited without pulling away from his gestures. We just sat there for maybe ten minutes. He nudged me with the arm around me to lean a bit on him, which I let him do. He leaned toward me and tilted his head so that it touched the top of mine. He began rubbing a place on my arm, just below my shoulder, very gently, very slowly. I didn't move away. I was waiting. His arm slipped a bit and his hand was on the tender place under my upper arm and he was rubbing there very slowly. A moment later his fingers were rubbing the side of my chest, where my breast starts. I did not want to move. I did not want him to think I wanted him to stop. I waited, totally immobile, wondering where the feeling would go. I was mesmerized, afraid it might disappear if I moved even a little, so I stayed very still. But he stopped and stood up and walked across the barnyard to the chicken coop, opened the door and went in.

I was quite stunned by the sensations he had provoked. I was unprepared and when I think about it, as I did often in the days afterwards, I knew quite clearly I was disappointed that it had stopped. I had not expected his caresses, but they had been welcome. I sat for a while on the straw in the barn's hollowness and then continued cleaning the barn. The children returned an hour or so later and we had our evening meal.

The farm routine continued as before.

TWO

During the first several weeks after the stranger came I went about my daily routine unchanged. I was very aware of his presence every minute of the day. I had no trouble assuming my usual behavior, I knew no other. There was very little that changed in my regular rounds and soon the stranger and his needs blended into the farm life. The essentials were giving him some food and emptying his bucket. I was not nervous about him being discovered, I felt detached, that if someone found him I would not be to blame, therefore I would not suffer for it. I did nothing, of course, to betray him. He was my secret and I did not want anyone to know about him, almost more out of my own selfishness than for his well-being. My protectiveness was quite total. I had no hesitation about it and nothing that happened later caused me any. I imagine that there was nothing in the way I did things that would have caused anyone to question me during that time.

One gets used, on a farm, to solitude. It isn't often that more than one person is needed to do a single task. Sometimes my husband would ask one of us to help with the seeding or the harvesting, but even then it's not like a common activity where you can converse or banter. Odd as it may seem, even the rather tedious task of placing the seeds in the furrow demands concentration. One cannot raise one's eyes to admire the sky or be distracted by a warbler. To be sure of efficient germination and proper spacing one must keep one's eyes focused on the furrow and the seeds, and later, when the plants emerge, one can always detect the places where one's attention wandered and the grain is crowded in certain spots. In any case, if I am seeding in this section it would be useless for my husband to be in the next row so as to be able to make idle conversation. We never had too much to talk about anyway.

Our people are serious about life. We have never had much to giggle about over the generations. Apart from the first year or so I mentioned earlier, my husband and I never found much to laugh about. When his needs were insistent he would follow the same ritual, as if it were written instructions. First he would place his hand on my left breast and massage it a bit. Then he would turn on his side and pull up my nightdress. He would fling his leg across my body and pull himself up onto me, and in a few moments it was over. Then he would fall asleep. There was very little way of knowing if he enjoyed it, though the enjoyment was not what you might call emotional, just physical. It was not in our way to enjoy things. After a while you could say it was some enjoyment just to finish our chores for the day. Still you knew you would have the same things to do when you woke up the next day. But these are farmers' customs. I doubt there's a farmer who isn't so busy with each day's chores that he can find the time for extra things. Sometimes I wondered what the porch had been built for, except to make some shade for the front room. We never had moments to sit on the porch to enjoy the air or to watch something going by on the road. When the children were small they oftentimes sat on the porch steps and used them for a table for their little games. Now and again I would have the idea of taking the beans to the front porch to fix them, but when the time came I just stood in the kitchen and hurried up to finish the job. Later I would say, "You see, I just forgot I meant to take those beans out to the front porch to tend to. Next time."

Very few visitors came out to the farm. We got deliveries from time to time, but often they would just drop the feed or whatever outside the barn and take off before we could notice they were there. Many's the time I would look up from my laundry and see the wagon pulling out and I'd never realized it had been. You can't really call these visitors, I suppose. If you did come for a visit, you would know, as my family knew, that you were keeping me from some chore that wanted doing. We didn't have the habit of exchanging visits back and forth, but if someone were to stop by the farm unannounced of a usual day they would not find us doing anything but our work. If you thought about it, there was a certain satisfaction in taking care of the animals and the fields, since they were dependent on your doing it every day. The poor critters needed you like the babies did. There was some feeling that your work was important; after all, who else would do it? Satisfaction is not the same as enjoyment and while you might smile when you have picked over the last of a hundred bean plants, part of the smile is gratitude that there aren't a hundred and one plants and part the congratulations that you give yourself when you finish something.

So, while I thought about the stranger all the time, I doubt there was any way a visitor might have known it. My thoughts did not show through on my face or in my demeanor at all. While you would see me humming as I crossed the barnyard to the chicken coop every day you wouldn't be likely to notice the food I was carrying with me, apart from the feed. We never exchanged any words between us. I just included him among my chores.

When my husband left for the army, I felt a certain calm within myself. He outlined what I must do to maintain ourselves. He was right that there would be more opportunity for eggs, and occasionally chickens, than milk or pigs or vegetables. I did not evaluate his recommendations in any way, I just carried them out without hesitation. I set about accomplishing the plan with enthusiasm for making it succeed. If it failed it would mean our way of life would change. In all the years of our farming together, since our marriage, I had spent my days in the privacy and seclusion of our farm, in the farmhouse, in the vegetable patch behind the house, in the barn and the chicken coop. That was my world. If you sat in the road from just before sunrise to the end of day, you would know as much about what I did as my husband. Certain days there was laundry, certain days there was putting by beans when they were ready. As the children grew they left me more time to tend the animals, but the chores were the same and they rose up every day just like I did. When my husband went off to the army, the children needed me less and the farm more. I began making the trip into the village every other day, Monday, Wednesday, Friday and then Saturday. Saturday was the market day, which meant I would take a few eggs, a chicken or two if there were any, and some vegetables and stand in the square with the other farmers, hoping to sell everything and carry home only some things I had taken in trade and some pfennigs. My husband had told me about market day only as a possibility, not knowing if it would be worth my time. Some of my customers had asked me why they never saw me at the market and I felt I shouldn't let an opportunity go by. So I tried it and found it more and more a success the more I understood how it worked. As I made my rounds during the weekdays, selling only eggs, I asked the housewives if they needed anything else I could provide. Sometimes they asked for a chicken or some potatoes and they said, bring it to the market and we'll have a look. So I did. The more prospects I lined up, the better it went. Gradually the market reflected the hard times that were overspreading the country. There was less produce available each week, and more customers wandering through fewer and fewer booths. I never developed much of a selling style. I let the housewives know my things were fit to eat and I tried to price them always a pfennig or two below the others. So from the beginning I went into the village four days out of the week. It was rare that I was not back on the farm by early afternoon. I would make the trip to the village in about an hour, but without anything to carry, the trip home was nearly half that.

These trips to the village introduced me to many new ways. After the first few weeks the other vendors no longer looked at me as a stranger, and I began to feel more comfortable among them. Even though I didn't exchange words with them, I became a familiar face and they began to expect me each week with my chickens and produce. Most of the vendors were women and old folks, not only because of the army call-ups, but because these were the ones who could be spared from Saturday chores. After so many years, these farm people had grown friendly and looked forward eagerly to their Saturday market meetings. The market, therefore, had a lively aspect, with constant shouts from one to another, arguments, usually playful, continuing from week to week, laughs and stories punctuated by customers demanding prices, and almost unwelcome interruptions to wrap a package or make change. From the vendors' point of view the customers were an inconvenience to their socializing, so that the most agile-tongued vendors would inject comments to browsing customers without really interrupting the flow of their gossip.

It was as though I had travelled to a new world where people spoke of things which I had no reference for. It took a while simply to figure out that the shrieks and yells were mostly good-humored banter. Vendors chided each other on the quality of their wares, sometimes belittling a head of cabbage or ridiculing a piece of cloth. After some weeks I heard them include me in their insults, mocking the size of my eggs. This was my initiation, my acceptance by them depending on how I reacted to this public display. I never felt so comfortable among them that I was moved to join in, but I didn't take offense and eventually the cadence of their calls provided a familiar background to the morning's sit in the square. The calling back and forth was like a barker announcing what was available in the market.

"Oh, here's the Egg Woman with a scrawny little cock to sell. No wonder she didn't want that skinny creature eating all the feed."

"Look at the pathetic peppers Mrs. So-and-So has brought today. Maybe there is someone who hasn't eaten in a week who might think them plump."

And so on.

The undercurrent to this loud shouting was a more intimate conversation on a more serious level. Several women circulated with news of the government food man's scheduled visits, of new restrictions or quotas that were expected to be imposed. Often those who had the same crops huddled together to agree on how they might get around some regulation or requirement. I heard in this way how to conceal dodging the milk usage restrictions. In this case, farmers were prohibited from keeping any milk for their own use. Since fat had disappeared almost completely from the market, making butter was a profitable sideline. In order to continue this activity, farmers watered down their milk to reach their usual quotas, after removing some for making butter. Even making butter for one's own use was not allowed, but every farmer I met did so anyway.

I kept myself from most of the others, attempting to blend in as much as possible, without calling attention to the fact that I was not actually involved. Many of the women in the market seemed to have self-appointed duties; they circulated among the booths, inspecting produce, selling government publications.

I did not have a habit of passing the time of day with the housewives who bought the eggs. On rare occasions one might remark on the weather, but more often they asked my price, asked how fresh the eggs were, and that was that. It was on market days that I began to exchange a few words with the other vendors. In general only the women would speak to me. They would usually complain about something, in most cases the weather or the Farm Bureau. Those were the two things the farmers depended on for their livelihood. These were the subjects farmers were most interested in in those days.

After a few weeks I became used to having the man hiding in the coop. He had never touched me since that time in the barn and there had been no further occasion for him to spend time in the house. Even though we had no conversations, I was pleased that he was there. I couldn't say specifically why, but it gave me pleasure to have my own secret, as if through this private act I could be in contact with things from beyond the farm. It was welcoming and embracing a world I didn't know, a special dramatic mysterious world that I could share in while this person was taking refuge, relying on my complicity, unknown to anyone at all, there in our chicken coop among the chickens.

I made no sign to him, I showed no outward change in my manner, I kept to my routine and my usual rather withdrawn attitude toward those around me. There was no discussion of his leaving since I had no need to broach the subject and he seemed content as things were.

One day as I was working in the far fields, the girl came to get me, saying the Gestapo was asking for me. She said an officer had driven up on his motorcycle and wanted to speak to me. I stifled an instant flash of fear, took control of myself and told the girl to go into the house to bring some schnapps for the officer and I went to speak to him. In the time it took me to walk to the road, I had completely composed myself.

"Good afternoon, sir," I said. "My daughter is bringing you something to drink. How nice of you to visit with us today."

"Thank you, my good woman, that is too kind of you." And as my daughter came from the house, "But really, this is too kind. Oh, the bottle is not even yet opened the first time. Really, I can't accept...."

"Of course you can, sir. Please open it and enjoy a nice drink. My husband left it for you and he would be very upset if he knew you came for a visit and I did not offer you something. Please have some."

The officer asked my daughter and me some questions about the farm, how many pigs we had and the like.

"I wonder if you like to eat a nice fresh egg now and then," I said. "Our chickens lay the best in the region. May I offer you one? One of our layers is four years old and still lays an occasional egg as big as your fist. Please let me get one for you, if we are lucky enough to find one of those." I surprised myself with my ability to chatter with this officer.

He followed me toward the chicken house, but just as we got to the gate of the enclosure, I said, "Sir, please, it is obvious you do not have chickens where you live. No one but me can go into the coop. The chickens are very nervous, they do not know you and perchance they may stop laying and my entire income will be lost. Let me see if I can find you a nice large egg or two." And with that I turned on my heel and walked purposefully toward the coop, hinging the gate behind me. The Gestapo man stood there, not terribly upset, with my daughter, drinking his schnapps, while I went to find him an egg. I went directly to the nests and searched around for a handful of eggs for the officer.

"This is quite a substantial assortment of eggs we found for you, sir," I told him when I returned. "Let me wrap them for you so that they won't break on your way." I led him and my daughter toward the house with my apronful of eggs and we all went inside. I found some clean rags to wrap the eggs with and presented them to the officer.

"This is most kind of you, ma'am. I notice that there is not much in the way of fresh eggs in most of the markets, so this will be a most welcome addition to our meals."

"You are most welcome and I hope that you will come back whenever you like for some more eggs. My husband, were he here, would be so pleased to meet you. He is serving in the army at this time."

"So your daughter has told me. Ach, I have nearly forgotten my official business. We are conducting a search in this area for an escaped prisoner. The Gestapo office in the next province has asked us to pursue this search as they have been unable to find the dog. He escaped a month or so ago from Mauernich camp and may still be in this area."

"Is he dangerous?"

"We don't know if he is armed, but the high Gestapo officials want him back. It could be they think he is anti-government. He may be hiding in the woods somewhere near here. If you do find him, please let us know."

"Certainly, sir." This from both myself and my daughter in unison.

"There is a generous bounty for whoever finds this escapee. We like to reward loyal, patriotic citizens whenever they help us find and punish the misfits and evildoers among us. I hope you will earn the bounty, good people."

The officer tucked the eggs under his arm and, with his high boots slightly dirtied from the barnyard accumulation, he strode into the front yard, mounted his motorcycle and rode off down the road.

My daughter was very excited about this visit. She said her Girls' group would be happy to hear about our contribution to the Gestapo, that we were part of the searching area for this escapee. She said she would spend some time from her schoolwork searching the high grass on the knoll in the back, in case she should find him hiding there. I agreed she should look there, but I suggested the weekend might be a better time to start. She liked the idea and was bubbling over about our farm's participation in the man hunt.

The next day when she, and the boy, had gone off to school, I went to the coop to see if he was still there and to tell him of this development. The day before, when I went into the coop looking for the eggs for the officer, I had purposely avoided glancing toward his usual place, making the job as brief as possible. I had been tempted to return to the coop on some excuse, but I hadn't wanted to raise questions by having the children discover me in the coop without reason, so I waited until the next morning. As I went into the coop, I could not see him in his spot under the roost and I began to panic. My first thought was that he had left and would be picked up by the Gestapo and returned to the camp. I felt that it would have been my fault since I hadn't gone to warn him. Not only that, but I knew most clearly that I did not want to have him leave. He was not under the roost and not visible in any other corner of the coop. The coop was not large enough to imagine anyone could be in it and not visible. It was only about four paces by four paces and only the nests on one side and the roost on the other. The feed and water were set up near the other wall and the rear wall was empty. When I didn't see him in the coop, I thought, if he has not left he may be in the barn or somewhere else, maybe even in the tall grass the girl had mentioned. Before I could leave to look for him, he was standing before me, drawing me toward him, hugging me in victory and triumph.

"We passed our first challenge. We did it. You were wonderful. I didn't know you had schnapps hidden away. You were splendid with the fool. 'You might frighten the birds and then they may never lay another egg.'" He imitated with a mincing voice the little half-deception I had used with the officer. "What a stroke of genius. What a performance."

"Where were you?" That was all I could get out. He was hugging me still and lifting me up off the ground.

"Come and I will show you." And he led me to the corner of the coop, under the roosts, where you had to bend low to squeeze into the corner. He pulled up a board and showed me where he had hollowed out a place underneath, quite an ample space, and showed me how he could get under and replace the board. When he was under there and the board was in place, there was no way of suspecting someone was there. The chickens scampered over the area, now so accustomed to him that they didn't get nervous.

I looked at him with open admiration as he showed me the place under the floorboard. It represented permanence, like a grave in the chicken coop, that would keep him there. "Were you under there when I came in to get the eggs?" I asked him.

"Yes, ma'am. I heard the motorcycle approach and decided that this was the first time I would need my hiding place, I call it my burial place, and I lifted the floorboard as I showed you and slipped in. When you came in for the eggs, I had already been in there for quite some time. But I heard everything you said and you were wonderful." Again he hugged me to him in exuberance at escaping the worst.

This event that presented so much in the way of danger for him, and for me, drew us closer together. Beyond merely allowing him to exist in the coop, I had protected him, actively shielded him. He had heard everything I said, he knew I had saved him. And he had revealed his secret hiding place, opening himself further to depending on my trust. I still had only a vague idea of what actually was going on. I knew he had escaped and was wanted for that. But what kind of place had he escaped from? Why had he been put there in the first place? I felt that my daughter may know more about these circumstances than I. I knew what my motivations were. I could be clear with myself that this man made me feel things I feared had been lost permanently.

It was as though he forgot that touching me would have any consequences, either for me or for himself, but when he hugged me so forcefully, I felt his nearness and he may have felt something similar since he looked at me and slowly lowered my feet to the ground and let me go. I took a step or two backwards and said, "I don't think he'll be back this way soon."

"Do you know why he wants me?"

"You told me yourself. You escaped from Mauernich camp."

"Do you know why I was in that camp?"

"You were refusing to leave the university."

"Why was I told to leave the university in the first place?"

"Your papers were not in order."

"Right. But what papers are these?"

"I don't know."

"Now we are getting somewhere finally. I will tell you. I owe it to you, because you saved my life and now you might change your mind about the whole bargain we have forged here so charmingly. I believe you do not know the real reason I had to leave the university. The papers I needed were birth certificates and I couldn't satisfy the authorities."

"You didn't have your birth certificate?"

"I did have it. I also had my parents' and my grand-parents'. I had to submit seven birth certificates and they all had to indicate that every one of us was Aryan. This I could not do."

"You are not Aryan?"

"No, I am Jewish."

"Oh."

"That is all?"

"Well, what should I say?"

"Do you know that Jewish people are not citizens? Do you know that Jews cannot attend the university, that they are not fit to be educated, that learning is only for Aryans?"

"No, I didn't know these things."

"Now you know them. Do you want me to leave? Do you know now what the danger is for you and your daughter and your son because I am hiding here in the chicken house?"

"No."

"If they found me here they would execute me on the spot. I have no rights whatever. You and your children would be taken away, put in a camp for political aberrants, your farm would be distributed to more loyal citizens and that would be the end of everything."

I could say nothing more. My head was buzzing with what he had told me. I had no idea of the circumstance he referred to. I looked at him and saw the distress in the lines of his face. What could be done? The dimensions of the situation had grown from what I had imagined. I had thought this person a runaway and instinctively I had refrained from giving him away. I could later see how completely I was given in that first moment of discovery the power to protect this stranger. I never thought about whether or not he was worth protecting. He never appeared to pose a danger to myself or the children. It was merely his presence, given into my power, that had to be secured, without question. I did not say, this is a criminal, this is a bad person, pursued by the authorities, we do not want him here. I said, here is a person who needs protection, we will protect him, I will protect him. Nothing further.

This news of being Jewish, a Jew, well, what did it change? This was the first Jew I had met and I had not even noticed until he told me. How should I have known? He seemed just a desperate person in need. I had no way to relate to this information. No one had told me to think about Jews. I knew there were Jews in the big cities, but what they did there or why they were a bother I did not know. I knew they were not liked particularly, but why, I had no idea. For me it was a problem of the cities, like telephones. I might have known about it had I lived in a city, but our talk was about our problems. Even in the village, certainly in these days that I was spending some time there, we spoke about surviving, we talked about evading the Farm Bureau regulations, we discussed our prospects. In none of these discussions was there mention of Jews.

When he told me these things about himself, I really had no preparation for it. In the same way that he had obviously not spent any time on farms and did not know what were the things that farmers do, I had not had any contact with Jews and did not know what they do. As I left him again in the coop, I sensed that he needed to hear me reconfirm my intentions, but I needed to think a bit about what he had told me. I was troubled, not by the news that he was Jewish, but by my ignorance of how best to react to this news. Now that he had warned me and revealed to me this information, I should somehow show him it did not matter to me and that I would continue to allow him to stay in the coop. Actually I had no doubts about him remaining in the coop, but I knew I did not fully understand what his being Jewish had to do with it.

I found that the following Saturday when I went to the market in the village square, the vendors were talking only of the Gestapo, who was looking everywhere for the escaped Jew. They all referred to him in this way. "Did the Gestapo stop at your place looking for the escaped Jew?" As soon as I heard this question being tossed from vendor to vendor, I relaxed totally. While they were jabbering about this mystery, I was sitting among them calmly with the answer, an outsider disguised as an ordinary vendor.

When I heard them discussing the Gestapo's visit, of course, I paid closer attention. They wondered nervously if one of them would wake up one day and find this escaped Jew on their farm. Their nervousness came both from the horror of having a Jew desecrate their own farm and worry about what the Gestapo might do to them if they were found to have the Jew, even if they reported it themselves to the Gestapo. There was no doubt that they would lose no time in reporting any escapee they found, since there was a bounty given to anyone who provided information that helped locate one. I looked around, listening to the gossiping about the escaped Jew, and realized that no one had the least suspicion that I might know. I, who harbored this escaped Jew in my own chicken coop, was among them and they had no way of detecting this about me.

That afternoon when I returned to the farm I was not able to talk with him because the children were at home. When the children were there, doing their chores or their schoolwork or Youth activities, I never made contact with him. I sometimes had to go to the chicken coop to gather eggs or feed the birds, but I never looked toward where he might be to see if he was there. I never checked his hiding spot. I did my best to forget that he might be there. I would hum my little tune for the chicks and know that he would be hearing it too. Sometimes I would see him as I tended the birds, but more often not. If I did see him I swept my glance over and away without a sign. He, too, never detained me at those times. He knew perfectly well when we were alone. The following day, Sunday, was the day the children went to their Youth meetings. They both left rather early in the day, rain or shine, and returned in time for dinner. So that day I went to the coop with the purpose of talking with him. As soon as I entered the door he approached me.

"Have you thought about what I told you?"

"I have thought of little else since."

"Probably I have made you risk enough already, I will make ready to leave during this next week."

"Judging from what they have to say about you in the market, you would not get very far from here without being reported. The talk is of nothing but how much the bounty will be. Where do you have in mind to go?"

"I don't know. You have been so kind to keep me here, probably it is time to give someone else a shiver of danger."

At that moment I felt jealous at the thought that he would pass into someone else's custody. I did not want to give that up. Beneath the jealousy were other, more confused, more urgent feelings that made it seem important that this escaped prisoner stay in my chicken coop.

"I would ask you to come to the house for a few hours to give you some change of scenery, but it's not safe. Do you know where you are? Did you have a plan when you came here?"

"Sure. I planned to save my neck. It had been a week since I escaped the camp and I had traveled only at night, eating practically nothing, drinking from the streams. I don't know where this farm is, but I made sure to travel west. When you found me I had spoken to no one but myself for a week and since then you have been my salvation. Every night I think about how long I should stay here, I think about the danger my presence holds for you and your family, and I wonder how long my luck will last. I think about leaving and how it will be when you come in the morning to find me and I will have left."

I could imagine the chill I would feel entering the chicken coop as usual and discovering him gone.

"Since you have stayed to now, it would be foolish to walk into the net they have set up for you in these parts. You would have made me endanger us all and then give it up. At least let us feel that we have seen you safely placed somewhere else. I should say, of course, it is not up to me to keep you here if you prefer to go. You should not be thinking about our safety, when it is for you that the Gestapo has set up a search party. It is you who must decide what is best."

"May I know your name?"

"Eva."

"My name is Nathanael. I want you to know everything. I cannot stay longer unless I am sure you know what you have under the floorboards of the chicken house. Eva, this is what happened: I was at Mauernich for a month. In that time I completely changed. Before this nonsense began I had been a gentle shy student. I rarely dared to speak with anyone, even my fellow students, because of my shyness. The moment they told me I could not continue at the university, I became already different. For me my life had been focused on studying and learning and becoming someday a professor to teach others. When they refused to let me enter the class, refused to let me into the library, refused to let me purchase the books I needed, I was like an animal. I had never been interested in politics, I am a mathematician, not a revolutionary, but when I went back to the university to retrieve my lecture notes and research papers, there was a rally going on at the gates. I to this day have no idea which party or which group sponsored that rally, but I decided to take a look and hear what the speakers were saying. As I approached the university gates the crowd was yelling some slogan that I could not understand and some others were yelling an opposing slogan, so that it was like a children's round, in which both slogans were present in the air at the same time and you could concentrate on listening to one or the other. As I got closer, someone from one of the groups became involved in a fight, either with one of his mates or someone from the opposing group. As if it had been a signal, a platoon of policemen on horseback descended from nowhere and began beating whoever they could reach with their crops. A few minutes after that another bunch of policemen, this time in vans, drove up and immediately began arresting everyone within their range. Those who could ran away, the rest were arrested and spent the night in jail, including me. The next morning I and one or two others, the only Jews in the group, were sent to the railroad station with a guard and we were escorted directly to the Mauernich camp. The month in the camp was perhaps more educational than all my years at the university. I learned many things that one day may be useful, but the most immediately useful lesson was how to sharpen a spoon.

"Once I had sharpened the spoon sufficiently—by the way, Eva, you may yourself need to know this detail, it is the handle one sharpens, not the bowl—I had to regress to the point where I could actually use it. It didn't take me long. The camp was not very well policed. You would easily be able to leave through the gates. But after a few steps the gunman on the watchtower would finish you off. Of course, I know this because I saw it happen a few times. I figured I would have to distract the guard before I went through the gate. This I did. I took my spoon-weapon and waited until the moon set one night and surprised myself with how quietly I could cross the camp ground and climb the watchtower. I surprised the guard and in effect put the spoon into his throat. I was in such a state of regression, totally possessed, that I only later, in reliving those moments, was able to appreciate the depravity of what I had done. I have judged my depravity to be the more serious compared to the guard's, since I was well aware that what I was doing was evil."

As he spoke this story, Nathanael, for he immediately had assumed his name in my thoughts, seemed to be recounting an incident he had experienced more than once. I think he had told this story in his mind often, as if, disbelieving that it had happened, retelling it would confirm its reality. Nathanael's horror at what he had done was plain. He did not seem curious at what my reaction might be, as if confident it would be identical to his own. The issue for me was more elemental, not a source of such obvious anguish. Killing the guard had been necessary for Nathanael's survival, not a matter to infect one's conscience.

"Nathanael, I am glad that you were smart enough to get out of the camp. Are you punishing yourself about the guard? Was there another way to do it? Would the guard not have done you in without a prick of conscience? Of course he would. You are disappointed in yourself, when you should be proud."

"We see things from a different side of the glass. While the guard looked at me and saw the equivalent of a dog, I looked at him and saw an equal. At the moment, only I have a problem."

I could not hope to console him on this matter and it was quickly apparent. Nathanael had told me this story as a sort of payment of a debt he felt toward me, not wanting to be beholden under false pretenses, so to speak. If he would accept my protection, he needed me to know what sort of person I was protecting. In fact Nathanael's story did not shock me, but his sensitivity and intensity were touching. Nathanael may have thought I would consider him unworthy of hiding once I had heard his story. I was not sheltering Nathanael because I judged him superior to others, but simply because the opportunity had arisen. This was not to denigrate Nathanael himself, but simply to explain to myself why I found his story irrelevant. My opinion of Nathanael did not change.

"Now that I know more of your story, do you think I will think less of you, Nathanael?"

"Do you?"

"Not at all. I admire your courage and determination. You have undergone much change in so little time. What else could you have done in that situation? Anyone else would have hoped to find within themselves the same courage you did."

"You don't mind harboring a killer like me in your chicken house?"

"Well, I don't really consider you a killer. You are very gentle and sensitive. If you were really a killer, you would have killed me long ago. But for some reason you trust me. I'm quite pleased about that."

"You ask me to decide whether to leave here now or to stay. I have told you my story because I want to stay. I believe I must stay here to survive. If I leave now, the Gestapo, already on the alert, will track me down in minutes. If I stay, I will have a chance. If I stay, you will be in peril, and your children, and your husband."

I saw the chain where he, in desperation, had enlisted my help, endangering me, and I, without a thought for the consequences, somehow pleased to do it, helped him, endangering my family, they unsuspecting. I knew without second thought that neither the children nor my husband would approve. I knew this so certainly that it never crossed my mind to enlighten any one of them at any time. I was protecting Nathanael from my children as much as from the Gestapo. The true terribleness of this did not occur to me until very much later.

Without much understanding of my own motivation I sought neither to terminate nor to share the fact of the stranger in my coop. In my mind was a mixture of trying to hide Nathanael for his own sake, the essential goal, after all, and keeping him as my own special secret. The risk I was running was quite secondary in my mind, though I accepted it. I think now I might have jeopardized Nathanael himself to keep him there, not that I would have wanted to.

"It would be foolhardy indeed to risk wandering about this area with the Gestapo on your trail. Common sense seems to be on the side of your staying in your floorboard hideaway. I can hardly be expected to stand by and wave goodbye to you at this moment, knowing you will be swept away to prison or worse. Really it would be quite unkind of you to ask it of me. At least let some time pass and see what develops. I will surely hear about it in the market if it seems safe again."

"You are so selfless, Eva. I will be spending the rest of my life trying to think of how to thank you. I agree it is more sensible to remain here for a while, if it is not too much to ask of you. Then as soon as you tell me the furor has subsided, I will continue on."

"Well, that's settled then." And before there could be further discussion I left him and went about my chores.

THREE

The work on the farm was becoming more and more arduous. The children, burdened with school work and increasing Youth group demands, were now doing less. The boy still brought the water in the morning, the girl tended some of the animals, but for me I still had the usual routines and new ones. The morning trek into the village three days and Saturday each week further cut into my chore time. There are times now when I look back to those days and with a startle realize how primitive the conditions were under which we lived. We had been born at the beginning of the century and were still under the influence of the previous one. Every week I baked bread, every week in the summer I put up food for the winter, every week in the winter I made soup, mainly from the table leavings and scraps, every week one day went for the laundry and another for the cleaning, once a week or every other we all took a bath, twice a month we did the books. Before my husband went to the army these tasks were mainly mine, but, aside from tending the children, I had only the eggs and the garden to keep up with. With myself the only adult on the farm, it was more of a burden. There were times when I felt a bit overwhelmed by the things that had to be done and at those times I became somewhat cranky. It was under such a cloud that I asked the children if they could take a larger role in the household chores. I suggested that one day a week they could devote entirely to farm chores. It was rare to find them unanimous about any issue, but they were firm and unhesitant about this one.

"Mother," the boy said, "you cannot expect me, with the possibility of becoming a leader in service to our country, to spend time tending pigs or picking beans. Our father is endangering his life to protect us and you complain about the small sacrifice you are asked to make. Clearly you are not aware of how your work contributes to the greater glory of our people."

"I realize you have been very busy these months, but where is it that you have been taught to leave the responsibility of the farm for the Youth group? Doesn't the group encourage you to help your family?"

"You have completely missed the point, Mother. It is just for the purpose of helping my family, and all the other families in the country, that I must develop my skills as a leader."

The goals of the Youth had become his and I would be hard-pressed to offer any plausible alternative. A similar response came from the girl.

"Now, Mother, how can you expect me to finish sewing my uniform and do your jobs too? Do you know what my teacher would say if he thought I was shirking my Youth activities? There are no excuses for such a thing. Really, they just throw you out of the club if you don't keep up. Of course, if that happens, there is an inquiry and I would simply die of embarrassment."

She was near the age I had been when I married. I had been a docile obedient child. She too was docile and obedient, but only regarding Youth group affairs. She had begged so to be permitted to join the club at the start. I remember her pleas about how all her friends were doing it and how the director of the school had come before them and encouraged them to participate and how they would be loyal citizens by joining. It was impossible to deny her desire to join, she indicated she would join even if she were not given permission. It was obvious that she would and so her father and I decided it was better to give the permission and the money for dues. The further argument had been that the boy had already been given permission to join the boys' Youth and she should also be allowed. So they both spent two hours after school each day and all day Saturday and sometimes Sunday as well in Youth group activities.

What they call the Great War had ended when my husband and I married. He had been under the age of call-up then. Of course, I knew we were at war, but really I knew nothing about it. Apart from school and helping on the farm, I had barely the time for my own private wonderings, without worrying about wars and faraway events. It was no relief when the war ended, except for those who had young ones that would no longer need to go into the army. In my growing-up years the war had been a constant in the background. We didn't read the newspapers much. Once a month or so, when my father went into the village he might bring back a page or two of some newspaper, often several weeks old and used to wrap lentils or some such. Mostly we were too busy to pay much attention to what might be in it.

We never really had the habit of inquiring about what might be going on some distance away. We thought about the things we were doing as we did them. We were taught to mind our own affairs and not interfere with what might be going on at our neighbor's. Well, this we did. Our awareness of what was going on in the large cities or some other country was as vague as it was of what was going on at the farm next door. When the stranger showed up in the chicken coop, it was the same as if a Chinaman had appeared. I had no idea why he came, where he had come from or what he was used to. I treated him in those first weeks as if he were indeed a Chinaman. I didn't think we would be able to communicate too well, so I didn't talk to him apart from did he need another blanket or the like. I felt as though maybe he didn't speak my same language, even though he obviously did. But I felt the foreignness of him, the differentness, and while it didn't frighten me—on the contrary it rather intrigued me—it did make me deal with him as an object, as someone whose feelings I couldn't begin to understand, so ignored. While I say he could have been a Chinaman, that's my way of saying he was not a farmer. When we wanted to describe something that was completely alien to our way we would say, That's how a Chinaman would do it, or Only a Chinaman would eat that, or That's an idea only a Chinaman would believe. Really, I found even the villagers strange to me. I couldn't conceive of living in the village, hearing other people's doors slam, people hurrying back and forth, clothes always ironed and matched. How city folk might be was what we heard tales about. Braggarts would try to show their worldliness by implying they had once visited the city and knew how to make their way around. Sometimes people would attempt to gain importance by claiming to have distant relatives living in the city somewhere, as though they had found the mystery of life thereby and had earned respect for it.

When the Gestapo came and Nathanael embraced me in excitement, it was the first time I had seen his similarity to me. Before then he was more like one of the animals I tended to than a real other human being. I never thought of betraying him before this time, but afterwards, I was more tenacious about being sure that it never would happen.

I maintained a cool and rather distant attitude toward Nathanael. Despite the fact that I liked having Nathanael in the chicken coop, I was reticent with him. Our contact so far had puzzled me. I did not know what to expect from Nathanael, so I thought it best to maintain a rather formal air, without expectations. It occurred to me that he might be bored with nothing to do, not to mention having to stay inside all day with the chickens pecking around. I thought he might help me with some of my chores. I brought a load of beans in my apron one morning. I asked Nathanael if he would like to string them for me as I had many other things to do and this needed to be done so that we could jar them up for the winter.

"I am so glad to do this for you. I wanted to ask if I could help you, but I was afraid you wouldn't want me to touch your things. Please, how do I do it?"

"You don't know?"

"No, ma'am, Eva. I am used to seeing beans already cooked on a plate with a bit of butter on top."

"I guess you had servants taking care of this scullery work. Well, on the farm we have to do it ourselves. It isn't at all difficult. Even a city boy can manage. Take the bean in one hand, pinch off the end, like this, and pull down the string that you find along this margin. The tips and strings go in one pile and the strung beans in another. The beans will be boiled for three minutes and put into jars. The tips and strings will go for soup."

Since he hadn't denied having servants, I guessed he really had, even though I had been joking. That was the joke we usually made when someone was lazy. "I guess we leave that for the servants to do, my pretty one." Probably he really had them. If you go to the university, would you have any time left over for chores? No doubt, one needed a servant or two if one lived in the city.

I watched him do a few beans and saw that he was agile enough at the task and that he could be left to it. I came back a short while later to find him still at it, but nearly finished. In this way I managed to find chores that Nathanael could do and that would help me run the farm. I brought some tools that needed cleaning, some baskets that had to be repaired and anything that might easily be carried to the coop and done there. After a few weeks we dared to have Nathanael do some picking in the garden, even though there was a small risk that someone would see him. You couldn't see behind the house from the road, you would have to be coming from over the rise, but I couldn't remember anyone ever doing that at all. So Nathanael helped me with the garden.

We talked very little. I feared alluding to something that he might interpret as wanting him to leave. Of course, every day I went into the chicken coop at least three times. In the morning, as I went to feed the chickens and gather the eggs, I brought Nathanael coffee and sometimes something else, if there was anything. In the afternoon I came again to check on the birds and bring Nathanael a bit of soup, some potato. In the evening, before sundown, I brought feed for the chicks, gathered eggs again and brought him dinner.

As I set aside things for Nathanael to do he became a more and more essential part of my day. As I thought of the chores ahead for the day, I ticked off in my mind ones I could pass to Nathanael. Vegetables that needed preparing for our soup, eggs that needed sorting or separating, even some mending I found less time for. So when I returned from delivering eggs, I often found several chores already completed. Actually, including chores that Nathanael did for me, I got credit for doing more than I could possibly have done. No one noticed and I complained to the children less than before, so they suspected nothing.

One afternoon, Nathanael was weeding the garden in the tomato rows and he called to me to come to see something. He held up a tomato caterpillar, green and fat, nearly as plump as the vines, and asked me what to do with it. I showed him how to slice it in half to be sure it was done for, and as I bent over this worm Nathanael gently put his hand around my shoulder and turned me towards him. I looked him in the face, and, seeing tenderness there, I leaned forward until we kissed. It was a tentative, soft, chaste sort of kiss. A kiss that marked the beginning of passion, but was in itself communication of another sort. This kiss, and I have thought many times since about it, was pure and questioning. It was Nathanael asking me if I would accept his kiss, if he could express his affection for me, if I was ready. It was me asking Nathanael if he would show me tenderness, if there was something going on within him comparable to what I felt, it was me wondering if Nathanael wanted what I did. Our lips meeting as they did, so lightly, carried us to a place where we could meet without being protector and escapee. Our kiss, irrevocable, acknowledged that what I had felt floating between us, the force that had left me without doubts regarding my hiding or not hiding Nathanael, was mutual and real. We exchanged our kiss with our eyes open, but our brows knit with questions.

Had Nathanael crushed me to him and raised my skirts in the rows between the tomatoes, I would have let him then. But after we kissed and separated, our eyes still on each other, his hands released me and he held me at arm's length. He saw that he had not overstepped my wishes, but some feeling of delicacy made him leave me and return to the chicken coop. I said nothing, but I wondered if my intensity had frightened him. I could not, however, pursue Nathanael, expose to him the desire I felt, it was not my usage. It was quite enough to have reciprocated the kiss, returned the pressure of his lips with mine own. That evening, after the children had returned and we had eaten dinner, I thought of taking a walk in the direction of the chicken coop, but the risk of the children possibly looking out their windows deterred me.

The next afternoon as I approached the chicken coop, Nathanael was just inside the door waiting for me. He drew me to him and kissed me hard on the mouth. My arms around him gave him the assurance he needed that I welcomed his touch and he kissed me on my neck below my ear, smoothing my hair and holding my head in his hands, kissing me on my face and seemingly everywhere at once. He carried me to his corner, where he had fixed the blanket I had given him, and laid me down on it. He found the places that needed touching and caressing and breathed in my hair and licked my ear and in a short time there was only moaning and sighing and breathing and sighing.

As I lay there later holding Nathanael's hand, I could barely recover from the surprise I felt. My body had been shaken so that it seemed to disintegrate for an instant and reconstitute itself piece by piece until I had returned to a state approaching normal. After a moment of realizing what had occurred, I turned to renew our union. Nathanael misunderstood at first and simply embraced me tightly until I said, "I want more, Nathanael." He held me apart, searching my face for my meaning, chuckled a bit and satisfied me again. When he felt my body relax, he held me close and caressed my hair and touched my body, my breasts, my nipples, kissing me and licking me slowly like a cat. He saw how my pleasure continued and he seemed pleased and mildly surprised that he could create this pleasure for me. "Have you yet had enough?" he asked me and I said, "No." He was amused and he continued, amazed that he had generated this extreme of feeling.

Each time my passion subsided a fraction I found I wanted it back, as if I doubted it had been there at all. There was a certain level that I had never before experienced and each time I found myself there I was stupefied. But I was making a discovery, through Nathanael, that exposed my innocence and limited experience.

"Have I been very selfish, Nathanael?" I asked.

"Marvelously so," he chuckled. "You haven't taken up the theatrical arts, have you? You can't be blasé, you don't mind letting me know I have you at my mercy?"

"It would never occur to me. Would you prefer me to hide myself from you? It might be more of a challenge for you. You perhaps would prefer to convince me, wheedle and beg me. Shall we start again, and I will refuse you for as long as you like. But I will not enjoy that game."

"Nor I."

We had been carrying on in the chicken coop for a comparatively short time and the chickens had begun to be curious. They began to gather around Nathanael and me as we sat up and looked at each other, laughing at the smiles we saw and the cackle that was growing around us. Intimacy with Nathanael seemed quite natural to me. Nathanael asked me once how it was that I didn't feel moral compunctions about such behavior. The experiences we had together were so easy and comfortable that they were the most normal part of our relationship. It was more unusual that on my own authority I had allowed him to stay in the chicken coop than that we had begun an intimate relationship. That was separate. Sharing pleasure with someone was not a moral issue. The subterfuge of bringing Nathanael food and covering his steps when necessary made me more nervous than the thought that we might be doing something wrong or that someone else might think so. I did not disguise for Nathanael the extent of my enjoyment, I sensed it was far greater than his. On some level perhaps there was an evening of debts, a power balance between us. Nathanael, possibly, saw this as a means of repaying his obligation to me.

Nathanael was an attentive lover. When he saw I had little experience, he set about to teach me what he knew. Our meetings were limited to the daylight hours when the children were in school. We took the time we could, but I did not abandon my usual routine. I continued to deliver eggs every other day and go to the market on Saturdays. This still left us a nice amount of time for ourselves.

FOUR

By midwinter, I had increased the sales of our eggs to almost double what it had been when my husband left for the army. My husband had outlined how to go about increasing our production and everything he had told me to do I had been able to do without difficulty. The demand for the eggs became more intense as time went on. Serious food shortages were beginning to show up even in the villages. The other vendors told me more people were living in the village now, people who were unhappy with what was going on in the cities and towns. There was never any lack of where to sell the eggs and it seemed as if each day someone indicated a new customer to me. One of my best customers had been with us since the early days, a woman who lived next to the church. This woman prepared meals for the priest and now that there were such shortages she frequently asked for a few more eggs. One day she asked me in, something she had never done before, and explained to me that the sisters in the convent needed eggs and an occasional chicken too. I could see no need for her secretiveness, but

I agreed to stop by the convent and take the order before I left for the day.

The convent was in the highest spot in the village, on a street that had no outlet except into the convent gates. From the front garden there was a direct view towards our farm, but there were too many trees in the way to actually see it. When I rang the bell at the gate I saw window curtains being pulled aside here and there, checking to see who had rung. Finally, one of the sisters came and let me in. She led me into the entryway, just inside the oversized wooden front door, and asked me to wait. There was an eerie breath in the silence as I stood looking at the fine carved wood around the walls and the colored glass windows reaching upwards several stories above me. Although there was a chair in two corners of the room, large heavy carved wooden chairs with spiral turned legs, I had no thought of sitting in them. They seemed to be specimens, showpieces, rather than for actual use, and other than these, there wasn't another thing in this room. I felt that I had intruded into a place of secret routines and mysterious rituals, where each moment of the day would have its own special act which an outsider could never get the significance of. Interrupted by a caller, the sisters were so polite and cordial that one would never know what they had broken off, to be resumed when the stranger had left. Polite as they were, you were never sure you hadn't inadvertently broken a rule, or, even worse, caused the sisters offense. There was always a fear that through some inexplicable misunderstanding you would be made to stay and join in the prayers and by some overwhelming power you would not know how to say that you wanted to leave and you would soon learn to know the ways and become a sister and believe. Centuries of prayers and years of belief circulated in the air of the room, belief that could be breathed in, vital parts sucked into all corners of one's body and exhaled to linger in this room for a few hundred years or so, only to be inhaled by another.

A large sister rustled the mystery in the air as she came in the entryway wiping her hands on a towel tucked inside the rough belt that gathered her ample habit at her waist. I supposed she was the cook. She introduced herself as Sister Karoline and asked me how many eggs I might bring on a weekly basis. I told her that the most we had ever collected in a week so far was about six dozen, but that by May there would be a lot more because we had kept more chicks. She said that was fine and would I bring her one dozen each week to start. I said I would and we settled on the price. She then gave me a box that she said she wanted me to put the eggs in. She wanted me to carry the eggs in the box and when she picked them up on market day she would give me another box for the next dozen in which I would find my payment each week. I had no objections to this arrangement and so I had my best and most steady customer.

The longer I frequented the market the more I learned. After the first Gestapo visit, I paid more attention to the gossip of the other vendors. At first I had ignored their chatting, since I had no context for it. The other women, especially, became accustomed to me and occasionally asked me about some matter or another, as they were asking the others. This was how I discovered that we were to expect a visit from the Farm Bureau man again. This man lived in a nearby village and it was his responsibility to visit all the farms in our area. He had been a schoolteacher and through political contacts had been appointed the local representative of the Farm Bureau. He had to supervise production and establish quotas. Any time the government had a new regulation he was supposed to see that it was followed and that people knew about it. He kept a record of our farm's activity, including the horses we used to have. When he visited us and learned we were increasing our egg production, he raised our quota for the flock and told us how to improve the feed we gave the chicks. The next time he came by he told us about a manure spreader that was available if we wanted to purchase it from another farm. It was rare to hear of any farm equipment available, since none was being manufactured and few people wanted to part even with old rusted machinery. Well, he explained, this was a pretty new machine, hardly ever used, since the people who got it found shortly after they bought it that they wouldn't be permitted to use it. We didn't question this further, understanding that we would benefit from someone else's misfortune, which we preferred not to know about in detail.

I was the only one who tended the chickens. When my husband came home for his leave he thought he was doing me a favor by gathering the eggs in the morning as he used to do. He made the birds so nervous that there were no eggs for a week. The birds were used to me and they seemed to like my way of caring for them. They let me inspect them and, especially with the older ones, I had no trouble making them do what I wanted. I was rather amazed in fact that the chickens didn't put up more of a fuss when the stranger came to stay in the coop. But in no time they became used to him being there.

The stranger, or, I should say, Nathanael, for that was how I called him in my thoughts, quickly became a part of my routine. I had only slightly been aware of the fantasy world that took up space in my mind as I went through the days of farm life. Yet Nathanael and his sweet attentions had displaced the mist of dreams of some unknown pleasures that were there to be enjoyed in that some-day world that would never be. There were occasions when even Nathanael seemed imaginary and as I lay in my bed thinking of our moments in the chicken coop a certain cloudy dreaminess softened the clear hard reality that Nathanael actually was and the sharp focused throb of delight that we shared. There was something tentative in the memory of our pleasure that wasn't at all there when we were together. There was always a moment when I wondered if Nathanael could make me feel that instant of levitating, of what cannot be described by such as me and had never been experienced by me before. There had been times when I had touched myself to see if there was life there still, but I had not found what Nathanael had brought and the feeling had been bitter and brief. With Nathanael there was a long lingering of his touch that remained with me throughout the day. Thoughts of Nathanael and our being together were now constantly humming in my head.

The chicken coop provided us privacy, at least from human interruption. As a rule, when we didn't want the chickens to bother us we would let down the cabbage ball. This was a device my husband had created to distract the chickens when they became aggressive towards another chick. This cabbage was hung from a string tied to the ceiling so that it would swing around and the chickens could attack it and peck at it instead of at each other. When the cabbage was hung out, the birds would flock around it and Nathanael and I could more or less be ignored, at least for a half hour or so. Sometimes when I came into the coop, I would find the cabbage already hanging and I would feel a rush inside to know that he had been thinking of our being together. He always waited for me in his corner, giving me the option of just going out again without acknowledging him as a safety measure that we understood without having ever discussed it. It was never necessary. Usually when I came in the coop, I made sure I didn't give myself away until I was under the roost, in the shadows where I and he could not be seen through the coop windows. There was never anyone who would look through those windows, but it was just a matter of precaution. By the time I got over to his corner he had already removed his clothes and set about removing mine. Sometimes I came to the coop without my underpants on as a surprise. When he reached under my skirt to remove my underpants and found I had none on, his delight was enormous and he pulled me to him without taking the time to take any of my clothes off at all. For a while that summer I took to not wearing any underpants and though I did not imagine we would have the occasion to be together as I was making dinner in the kitchen or hanging out the clothes to dry, for me it was a private reminder and I continued to do it. The feeling of the air coming between my legs as I went about my day was exciting to me.

Our meetings then were limited to the daytime hours. New fuel for the fires of our passion we found in conversation about our sensations. It's hard to describe such conversations, but mostly we talked about our being together. What there was to these discussions escapes me now, but we never strayed to anything but our present. The past, a time when we had shared nothing, seemed irrelevant and the future was never imaginable except as a continuation of the present. We luxuriated in these moments of murmuring; at least for me, this was the only time in my life when I and another were thinking of the giving of pleasure and thereby receiving it. We were like children in a game, discovering the possibilities, amazing each other with invention and delighting in the privacy of its secretness. It was the first time that I had ever spoken with anyone else of my feelings.

Every so often I received a letter from my husband, usually to remind me about something I should be tending to on the farm. I never thought of him in danger or what he might be doing. His being in the army meant for me that he was not on the farm. I understood it was obligatory and that it related in some way to the war, but I did not know where he would be fighting or who. I would in turn write to my husband, telling him how many eggs we were selling and whatever else was happening on the farm and with the children. My husband seemed pleased with the way we were maintaining our lives without him.

One evening at dinner the children were gossiping as usual about school friends, normally a subject I paid no attention to since I didn't know who they referred to. This time I was shocked into alertness.

"...she found out that he was mixed and she was picked up. It seems one of the other girls told the authorities about it, probably out of jealousy."

"What did they do with her?" the boy asked.

"They sent her to a camp for reeducation. She didn't want to go and she made all sorts of promises, but in the end there was nothing she or her family could do. She admitted that she had slept with the snake during her work year in the city and insisted that he had hidden his mixed blood from her. Shouldn't she have known?"

"You would think so. How disgusting to think she would have dirtied herself so. No one will ever go with her. In fact, I thought they would take care of her."

"What do you mean?"

"Well, there is a permanent punishment for such a repulsive crime."

"Like what?" she persisted.

"You know."

"You mean—"

"Of course."

"What do you mean, children? What punishment was it?" I asked, drawn to their conversation, but completely confused.

"Why, Mother, we can't speak of such things with you," the girl said in embarrassment. They had ignored me during this exchange since they assumed I had no idea about or interest in whatever they were discussing.

"Well, you have brought me this far. How can you leave me hanging without knowing her punishment? You must keep me up to date."

"But, Mamma, these are not things we can share with you," the boy insisted.

"Surely this is not so shocking that I will not be able to grasp it. Give me a chance. I should know about what's going on too."

The girl whispered, "They are going to sterilize Elisabeth because she had relations with a boy who has a Jewish grandfather."

"Sterilize?" I whispered back.

"Yes, Mother," the boy explained. "They will be sure that she will never bear children and that in effect she will never marry. Anyone who would have relations with such a person cannot be trusted to reproduce for our country. She has undergone some sort of mental collapse to do such a thing and she is not stable enough to bear children to serve our leader."

I was completely shocked. I asked no further questions because I could not trust myself to maintain my composure. They explained this to me with such evenness, without a sense of complaint, with the idea of describing a quite fair regulation, as if they were discussing the mixture of wheat to corn for the chickens. The enormity of what they told me grew as I had time to think about it. It was even more horrifying when I considered how simply they accepted the justness of the punishment for the crime. Evidently this was something they were being taught in the Youth. How could they have thought of it otherwise? They have never had the opportunity of meeting a mixed-blood person, a Jew or any other. In our neighborhood there are only regular people, all the same, just like us. How would they imagine the parentage of the person they would be having relations with? What would they think of me?

The following day after the children had gone off to school I went immediately to the chicken coop, completely outside of my normal schedule. I was so preoccupied with the thought of what the children had told me that I even neglected my usual humming announcement of my entrance into the coop. I surprised Nathanael and the hens and he immediately thought I was bringing a message of imminent danger and began to take the floorboards up to hide himself. I told him that wasn't necessary and tried to shoo the chickens onto the porch so they would stop their noise.

"Your face is lined with tales of horror and fear has colored your cheeks, your eyes are beautiful with fury and anger, your nostrils are—"

"No need to quote poetry, Nathanael, this is serious. You will not believe what Olga and Karl have told me. They are sterilizing young people for making love with Jews. In this case it is not even a whole Jew, only a mixed blood. But they have taken her away and sterilized her, and she is only sixteen. She will never be allowed to marry and she will never have children. What has happened to allow this?"

"I am always surprised at what information has eluded you, my Eva. You are so innocent and pure that you do not even know what is going on around you. You cannot behave properly if you do not know what you are supposed to do and think. You have been violating one of the laws by being with me here under the roost. You have been fornicating with a Jew. For this the punishment is worse than mere sterilization, you know. After they have sterilized you a notice is posted on the public square so that you will be shunned by everyone and will no longer be able to sell your eggs in the village. Not because you are sterilized, of course, but because no one would trade with an antisocial element, for fear they would be labeled as a sympathizer. They would be suspect for buying your eggs. If you think you can then go elsewhere and begin anew you are mistaken because you must always show your identity papers, which will be stamped to indicate your punishment and that you should be ignored and treated as an outcast for the rest of your life. It will amount to being a Jew just making love with one. I see the grand confusion on your face. Please think about this and let's discuss it tomorrow when you are clear."

"I don't need to think about it. When have they decided they can tell me with whom I may make love? May I make love with a Chinaman, but not a Jew? What is this disease of the Jews? Do they fear I might catch it? Suppose they make up some other decree that they like but I do not. What will I do? They don't like to make love to Jews. That will be for them. For me, I will do as pleases me."

There was no hesitation in this decision for me, even though I understood that it was a serious matter. Perhaps the other Jews in the world were different from Nathanael. Perhaps Nathanael was an exception. There may be something about Jews that poses a danger in fact to the general populace and may be carried on in another generation requiring such a drastic law. This I didn't know. Nathanael had no obvious negative characteristics and had many rather endearing ones. I could not say for every one, but I could say for Nathanael that there was no reason for such a law. For the state to actually pass a law about who was to be slept with and who not seemed quite unusual. I could not think of another law I may have broken. Allowing Nathanael to stay in hiding in the chicken coop might be considered against the law. That having relations with someone could be illegal was a new concept for me.

Ironic, too. Thoughts about violating my marriage vows by being with Nathanael had occurred to me, but not because he was Jewish. You could say that my ignorance was so total that his being Jewish was to me an irrelevancy. I was unable to understand what bearing it had on his character or anything else. Why they had singled out the Jews was not clear to me. It is true that in my ignorance I continued to enjoy being with Nathanael, even after learning the risk I ran of being sterilized. Once Nathanael asked me if it heightened my enjoyment to know that he was wanted by the authorities, that he was a criminal. I laughed, because he was clearly not at all a criminal in the usual sense, even though he had escaped the camp and killed the guard. To me Nathanael had been arbitrarily declared a criminal, as I might have been had they decided egg farmers were criminals. It was more logical for Nathanael to be called upon to make laws than to be the victim of them. Now Nathanael asked me if on top of being with a criminal and a Jew, was it titillating to me that I myself ran the risk of punishment. I told Nathanael quite simply that what excited me was the way he looked at me, the way he touched me, the way I felt together with him. I cannot really analyze what was so special about Nathanael that granted me such pleasure, but I suspect it was the fact that no one before had thought of giving me pleasure, rather than taking it. My husband had presented my only other opportunity for lovemaking and his upbringing had not included concern for giving pleasure. Possibly for Nathanael it had been instinctive, or maybe it had been the circumstances, but certainly it was so that he seemed to react to the pleasure he saw in me.

I asked Nathanael what other surprises he could tell me, before I heard them from my children. He said there might be other things I didn't know, but he didn't want to be the one to tell me. I felt sheltered, but I had learned nothing to make me want to change. It was plain that people from the city, like Nathanael, had no clear idea of how it was to live on a farm, so maybe there was a sort of mutual ignorance that should be maintained. So far I had no reason to be anxious to take up city life, if it inspired such senseless rules.

I was troubled that the children had adopted this thinking without hesitation. What they deplored about the situation was that the girl had committed the crime, not that it had been a crime at all. The children adopted everything they were told in the Youth group. They reinforced one another when they discussed these things at home and tried to outdo each other in their loyalty and fervor to the leader and the country. Everything they did was done with the rationale that it was for the good of the country; if one opposed it, one opposed the country and was disloyal. That would mean the authorities should be informed and the person, even me, I thought, should be reported. I had little doubt that the children would report me without a second thought if they knew.

The children were at the age when it was not completely unexpected for them to feel an urgency to be on their own. In the cities perhaps young folk stay more at home, while they continue their studies at the university or become apprentice to some tradesman, but on the farm they were getting to the age where one thinks of marrying and setting up on one's own. A sense of estrangement was developing between us, as though they were becoming separate within the fragmented family that we were. With my husband away it may have been up to me to establish a liaison for my daughter and to encourage my son to find a wife. I took my daughter aside one evening and raised the subject with her.

"Olga, my daughter, I have been wondering if you are preparing yourself for marriage. At your age I was nearly a wife already. So many men are in the army, your father is not at home, do you have an idea of who you would like to marry?"

"Mammina, you embarrass me. It's more likely that I'll find a suitable mate in the Youth group than that you or Poppa should find me one. It doesn't seem likely that I will find a man on a farm near here since many of the farms are poorer than ours. On my work year in the city I will find a home where I can live and work and send some money home to you. This is what many of my friends are doing. Then for marrying they are finding men in the city, often soldiers or policemen. What do you think?"

"I will write to your father and see what his impression is as far as what would be best for you. Perhaps you would find some work in the village. I might make some inquiries among my customers and see what there is available."

I could see that Olga had already made up her mind to find work in the city, even though she didn't argue with my suggestions. I was naturally skeptical about sending her off to the city where her friends were having experiences as she had described. Who knew what else might be happening that I did not yet know about?

FIVE

Nathanael became very attached to the birds, particularly as the chicks began hatching. Because he had nothing to do he would occasionally pick up one of the smaller chicks and talk to it, smoothing its feathers. The other chicks would become jealous and crowd around as if they wanted some attention as well. I wouldn't say that the chickens became truly domesticated, but they knew Nathanael and after a while took him very much for granted, accepting him as part of their life in the chicken coop. The chicks that had known Nathanael since they were hatched were quite at ease with him. Nathanael was alone so much of the day, he made the chickens into companions of a sort. There were times when it was helpful having Nathanael there to mediate if the chickens started ganging up on each other. He told me that he saved one of the birds by throwing her out the window when the others found a tiny spot of blood on her after she had laid her egg. They began to peck at the spot and, liking the taste, the spot was soon gone and there was only her flesh and lots more blood, and more of the birds began to notice what was going on so that there were ten or more birds fighting over this poor hen. Nathanael had never seen anything like it before and he ran around chasing the pathetic bloody chicken causing great confusion among the others and finally managing to grab the chicken with both hands around it and toss it out the window. He had done the right thing, of course, because the bird would have been a goner, pecked to death in an hour. I tried to teach Nathanael how to use the hook, but he wasn't really interested in catching birds that didn't want to be caught. He had no trouble picking up the little chicks and holding them in his large hands.

At least once a week I would check over the chickens. I would see if there were any signs of sickness on any of them. If their color was changing or I could see anything unusual about them, I would grab the hook and drag the bird toward me and pick her up in my hand. I would then go over the five-point check that the Farm Bureau man had ordered. I would check the legs, vent, eyes, comb and wattle. If there was anything suspicious about the animal, if its color had started to bleach out, if its eyes looked puffy and bulgy, I would isolate it in a small wire cage that I kept for that purpose. I kept the cage in the barn and I fed that chick separately in case it was sick. Half the time I would put the bird back into the coop and the rest of the time I would either take it to market with me on Saturday or dispose of it if it were really sick.

Nathanael hated this procedure, knowing that the end result might be that one of his housemates would be selected out of the flock. Sometimes he tried to hide the chicken hook from me to make it harder for me to catch the birds. He tried to impede me from inspecting the hens and once he tried to hide a bird that had something wrong with its eyes.

The chickens that I set aside in the cage I would inspect on Saturday morning before going to market. I would collect the eggs that I planned to take with me, packed up nicely. If anyone had mentioned during the week that they would be able to use a chicken for Sunday dinner I would make a special effort to bring at least one with me. This was what Nathanael tried to prevent. He did not even like me cooking the chickens for our own dinners.

"Can't you see the situation I'm in. I have to sit among these birds all day and then you expect me to enjoy eating one of them. You come and go and can be more heartless about it—after all, they are only animals. But when was the last chicken dinner you ate in the chicken house?"

I ascribed Nathanael's attitude to his urban upbringing. He could not look at the chickens as egg factories, he saw them as more like living animals than producing machines. When you live on a farm, I guess these thoughts never present themselves. But the Farm Bureau representative made his regular visits to the farm and he had to satisfy himself that the birds were healthy and that I was taking care of them correctly. Occasionally he would inspect the coop, he would peek in the door and maybe take a step in, but he never had the least suspicion of looking for anyone. He merely glanced at the nests, checked over the water trough and saw that the feed was uncontaminated. Sometimes the Farm Bureau man gave me suggestions for doing something differently, but he was most angry if he noticed any sick chickens among the flock.

The representative was pleased that I had increased the flock and that I had always more and more customers for the eggs. I was getting more business from the convent. That first week they requested one dozen eggs. After a while they gave me a bigger box with twice the money in it and I brought two dozen the following week. Eventually they increased the amount again and sometimes they would ask me if I had any chickens. By summertime, they were buying three dozen and at least a chicken each week, sometimes two.

It was Nathanael who asked me about the convent. "How many nuns do they have living there that they can eat so many eggs?" I had no idea at all, and it wasn't my way to make such inquiries. Yet, fortunate as it was for me, it was odd that there should be such a sudden increase in their need for eggs. When I asked Sister Karoline as casually as I could if the sisters were enjoying the eggs, she said something strange. She said, "It's for the children." I didn't know there were any children at the convent and I imagined the sisters were looking after some orphans somewhere. Many families had increased their use of eggs since there was such a shortage of other nutritional things to eat. As I wrote to my husband, the general shortages were keeping us alive. We could sell everything I brought to the market. I almost never came home with anything. Everyone wanted fresh vegetables and had I been able to bring more things, I would have been able to sell them. There was very little meat in the shops in the village, I was told, and many of the villagers felt that eggs would replace the value of meat.

I still wondered about what children might be enjoying the eggs we sold to the convent every week. At the market I sat, my baskets at my feet, on a box I borrowed from the cafe, the chickens tied to my ankle with a string. When a customer came along to look over my things, I would stand up and wait until he or she had had a chance for a good look. I never made it seem that I was overanxious for them to buy from me. I tried to make myself as inconspicuous as possible, even though many of the other vendors were much more aggressive. At the beginning I sold very little because the villagers weren't used to me, but as time went by they came to appreciate my style of allowing them to decide if they wanted to buy my things, and they did buy them.

Just before harvest time, the Farm Bureau representative came by and told us there was a new regulation forbidding the use of wheat for the animals. Wheat and rye were to be exclusively used for the state as these grains were needed for bread for the army. We had tended the field carefully with the idea that it would provide good feed for the chicks as we expanded the flock. Without the wheat, we would have to spend money for the feed. When I asked the Bureau man what I should give these chickens, he told me he would sell me acceptable feed each month. We argued a bit about the price and he told me he would see if he could arrange for a loan based on the eggs and chickens I would sell. I told him I didn't want to go into debt to buy feed that I could raise myself. He pointed out that I couldn't use what I had already planted or I would be arrested, and that since it was treason I would probably lose the farm and my children would lose their mother. It was not my habit to argue with the Farm Bureau man, but this particular regulation seemed so outrageous and contradictory that I persisted. The Farm Bureau man looked hard at me as I began what I thought was a logical argument about feeding the chickens with what we were able to raise on our farm and he said, "I suggest that you think about what you have said. I'll forget that you said it if you like. I'll be back next week with the papers for your loan to purchase feed for the chickens."

That evening I told the children what the Farm Bureau representative had said. At first they too raised their eyebrows at having to give up our wheat, which had required so many hours of our labor and so much difficulty. In all our minds was what my husband would say when he heard, after his careful planning and preparing. After a brief moment, when I mentioned that I would be in danger of arrest for treason if I used it, the boy said, "Well, Mamma, he's right. I remember now, we were told that these grains were being collected and saved to support the army. Now we'll be feeding our father and the troops. We have to do our share in our quest for independence. Why should we give to the chickens what we should be giving to the soldiers? Actually, it would be the same as giving help to our enemies."

"What then should I give these chickens if they're to make any eggs? Does the state not want them to give us eggs? Up to now the Farm Bureau man was so happy that our chicks were giving us so many eggs. Now we must go into debt, which your father will not appreciate, in order to buy other feed. And who knows if they'll like it."

"Mamma, you must do what they tell you or you will put yourself against the state. You know that they know better than you do what is best for us all. Just thinking you can decide for yourself what to feed the chickens is treasonous." I could hear an edge in his voice, as if he had pulled a switch and he was merely reciting, not talking with me. Underneath his words I sensed an antagonist, not an ally. I decided to end the discussion.

"Of course, I must do as they say. How do you think we'll explain this to your father? Only we will worry about our chickens producing fewer eggs. How will we be able to afford this loan for the feed?"

"Mother, you mustn't let anyone hear you speak this way. They will not waste any time reporting you to the authorities." This he said in his new voice, he was speaking as a leader, a protector of the state, one who follows rules. Now I was talking to a model member of the Youth group.

"You're quite right, son. How foolish of me."

As I wrote to my husband, we had to go into debt to feed the chickens.

When the time came that fall to bring in the harvest that we had to hand over to the state to feed the army, I carried out the harvesting alone. Our field was not more than two acres and it had always been enough for the chickens with some little bit we could use for our own flour needs. This particular year I was determined that rather than have both us and the chickens do without, I would keep a portion of the harvest to one side. I took some old sheets from the storage chest and spread them out and piled some wheat grain in the middle and dragged it under the porch, where I knew no one ever went. In this way I kept about a quarter of the harvest and covered it with a sheet. From time to time I would replenish our old supply, which we had been allowed to keep, and I augmented the chickens' feed with it and used some for our own needs.

Nathanael was the first to notice the change in the chickens. He told me that some of the chickens seemed droopy and indolent, they let him pick them up with no fuss and they weren't laying at all. I put some of the ones he pointed out in isolation and over the next week saw that they were going into their molt. This meant they would stop laying for a month or two at a minimum. I had to record this drop in production on my farm card and submit it to the Farm Bureau man when he came. He told me I would be able to counteract this by keeping a light on in the coop to lengthen the day for the birds making them lay more eggs. Since we were well into autumn I had to get up about five in the morning to light the lamp for the chicks. I often wished Nathanael could have taken over this chore, but of course that was out of the question. So all through that winter we gave the chickens twelve or thirteen hours of light, and they did give us more eggs. Thanks in good measure to Nathanael, I was able to keep our egg quota nearly at what it had been despite the change in their food. Nathanael kept the peace among the chicks, so we didn't lose any more because of fighting or cannibalism attacks. He tried to make sure that all the birds got a good share of the feed, since some of them victimized the smaller ones or the weaker ones. Nathanael walked the floor of the coop as if he were a guard supervising their behavior. He used little mincing steps, partly in imitation of the chicken's scratching style and partly because it would only have taken two or three large strides for Nathanael to have covered the length of the coop. He spoke to them and when he did his voice rose in pitch and it sounded as if he were speaking to a child or a foreigner. The chicks seemed to listen.

I wasn't able to keep up with the demand for the eggs. I went to the convent first, my biggest customer. I told Sister Karoline that we wouldn't be able to keep up with the usual order. Her reaction was very strong, she was extremely distressed and did not try to hide it from me. It was as if I had been one thing she could depend on and now I was adding to her problems. "What do they expect me to do? How can we feed ourselves when there is no food? We need more than potatoes to live on. What do you eat, Egg Woman?"

"Well, we're allowed to eat what we need out of what we grow."

"I see." She said this with such resignation and sadness as if hearing a sentence of death, as if she had just lost her final hope.

Something about the sister's reaction stung me deeply and I felt as though in some way I were personally responsible for the maintenance of the convent and I had disappointed them. From then on, even if I had to go to market with no eggs, I made sure to meet the convent's order. Sometimes I added some greens too.

The Bureau man came on a regular basis and spent an hour or so filling in my card and his file booklet.

"How many this month, Ma'am?"

"Three hundred fourteen, sir."

"I know October is a low producing month, Ma'am, but I wonder if you're going to be able to make the quota for the year. What do you think, ma'am?"

"I'm doing my best, sir. We have a rather young flock as you know. We are only now keeping more at laying and that will increase our production. This was how you and I planned. Last month we began to burn the oil lamp to wake them up earlier and keep the day at the half and half point. Still the older birds produce less, and some of the younger ones nothing at all for a few months more. There is little I can do about it."

"How is your disease control?"

"We have no disease, sir."

"None at all?"

"No, sir. Would you like to see for yourself?"

"No, thank you, ma'am. Perhaps next month we can have a look, but today I'm in rather a rush."

"Still, sir, I'd like you to sample some of our eggs, just to see why they are so popular with the market customers. Perhaps you have heard the reputation they have developed?"

"This I would be pleased to agree to. I have had occasion to hear that your eggs are superior. What accounts for it, Ma'am?"

"My hens are happy, sir. This is my opinion. Happy hens must give tasty eggs. I have set aside some here from my older birds. They don't lay many, but they are large when they do."

"You may be a bit whimsical, but I suppose that's as good a reason as any. You know you will be a credit to your husband if you can raise your production of eggs. There is a rather serious shortage of eggs in the country and we will have no trouble finding outlets for as many as we can get. The price has been set so you know you will get a good return. You will be aiding the state with every egg that your happy hens produce. In this way you are also aiding the army. Do you know that we are attempting to achieve self-sufficiency? We want to depend on no one else for the food we need. You will be one of the heroes of the country if you increase your egg production."

"I hate to think the country depends on me or my chickens for such a goal, but I am dependent on selling these eggs for our livelihood. Of course, I would be happy to increase our egg production, for the state and for myself."

"Why you have given me at least two dozen in this carton, that's too much."

"No, no, I want you to know that my eggs are good. You can boil some, have some in an omelet and have some left over for perhaps a cake."

"Thank you, ma'am, the missus and I appreciate it. I'm sure we will enjoy them all."

I knew the Bureau supervisor was collecting from every farm he visited. It was only logical. He was going to need new clothes before long, with all the foodstuffs he was gathering every day. Everyone was making down payments, especially after the story made the rounds about a farmer who was forced off his farm.

After the supervisor left I went into the coop to tell Nathanael what had been said. There was no other adult I could trust to talk to. I had Nathanael captive in a sense and I knew he would not betray me if I was not enthusiastic about some regulation or other. Only with Nathanael could I speak as I thought.

"We're going to have to improve this flock, Nathanael. Will you help me do it?"

"What do I do?"

"I will teach you how to judge these birds. Since we have expanded our flock over this last year, we have more birds to look after, and you can help me check them. You see this one?"

As I spoke I grabbed a bird with the chicken hook and dragged her over to me and picked her up quickly. I held her in the palm of my hand and felt her up and down, checked her size, looked at her vent and in about twenty seconds had her down on the floor again.

"That one's okay, I guess."

"Wait a minute, what did you do? You didn't show me anything. I still don't know how to pick these critters up."

"Nathanael, I always forget that you came from the moon. Look, grab hold of the wing and fit your hand in between the legs like this and lift her up."

Nathanael tried to copy what I did and very clumsily scared most of the chickens over to the other side of the coop. I dragged another one over with the chicken hook curled around her legs and showed him again how to do it. I wasn't the best teacher, since to me it was like showing someone how to sit down, all you have to do is do it and you would learn. I was astounded by Nathanael's total ignorance of these farm things, as he called them.

"Probably you'll scare the chickens out of laying before you learn how to pick them up. Are you or are they more scared?"

"Go about your business now and I'll learn how to pick my roommates up."

Well, eventually Nathanael did learn how to pick up and examine the birds, and it was he who called my attention to one of the birds who was sick. Fortunately, I was able to get rid of it before the others caught the sickness from her. With Nathanael checking the birds, a rather tedious task, I was able to set aside for sale only those birds that we didn't want for breeding. We had to be very careful to keep the flock in quality. We did not want deformities, we did not want poor layers, we did not want boarders. I told Nathanael, one boarder in the chicken coop was enough.

Nathanael had a special feeling for his roommates, as he called them. He had certain favorites he particularly cared for, treating them to some of the bread crumbs that stuck to his clothes after his meal. He would let the little ones walk on his chest and peck up the few crumbs that fell as he ate. Once I peeked through the window and saw him holding himself still so that one little chick could get the crumbs out of his beard. Nathanael often picked them up and petted them, though I don't think they liked that so well, but they tolerated it from him. After he learned to pick them up, he developed a closer relationship with the chickens. He bustled among them, conscientious about watching them, and watching out for them. One day I found a chicken in his hiding place under the floor. When I asked Nathanael why he had put her there, he told me he wanted to protect her. As soon as I picked her up I saw why. The hen was scrawny, bowlegged and weird-feathered. This bird was destined for a trip to the market, but Nathanael had developed some sort of attachment to her and didn't want to let her go.

"Nathanael, what can I do with you?"

"I am your slave."

"Seriously, Nathanael. You can't work against me. You know how much we're paying for feed. You know the Bureau man will be back for an egg count. You know we are supposed to be improving the flock. How many others do you have hidden?"

"How will you punish me if you find out?"

Nathanael always knew what to say to me. I was always free to tell him to leave. That is, hypothetically, I was. To speak to him as though he had similar freedom was to bring on myself this response to remind me how dependent he was on me. He didn't really know, and I didn't really know, how dependent I was on him. I did not choose to examine either side of that question. In bed some nights I wanted Nathanael beside me. I thought of him in the chicken coop. I knew he was safe, but I thought how uncomfortable he must be. The time was nearing when the children were to leave for their work year and I thought about that.

I picked up the hen Nathanael had hidden and took her out to the isolation pen until market day.

At the market there was a woman who had introduced herself on the first day I had appeared. She explained that she was the delegate from the Farm Women's Group. She asked me if I wanted to join. When I said no, she reacted with surprise as if it were the first refusal she had heard. She explained that I would get valuable information and support from the group, but I continued to decline. She sought me out from time to time and tried to sell me a newspaper. I refused to buy it, telling her that I had no time to read it. She was offended actually, letting me know that since there was information in the newspaper, I should make time to read it so that I could run the farm better. I saw that she made her rounds among the vendors and it seemed that she was quite successful in selling her paper, most of the others bought one.

When the Farm Bureau man came one month he showed me my farm card and asked me about my work card. I showed it to him and he looked it over front and back and looked up at me with a quizzical look as if he was sure something was missing. "Why, there must be an error on your card, I don't see your membership in the Farm Women's Group."

"No," I said, "it's not an error. I don't belong to that group."

Now he was completely shocked and his eyes opened large and he said, "But you cannot be a woman working on this farm and not belong to the Farm Women's Group. How can you know what is expected of farm women? This is the only way you can do your duty as a farm woman."

"I thought I was doing my duty as it is," I responded. I did not want to argue with this person, but I also did not want to join the group. I didn't raise my voice in any way, I simply told my true feelings.

"Ah, but you haven't understood. Farm women belong to the Farm Women's Group. It's as simple as that. If you do not join, the delegate from the Farm Women's Group will have to report that there is one farm woman in her area who refuses to join. She will be admonished by her superiors and our entire district will be considered with suspicion. You will find that difficulties will arise for you. The next time I come to renew the feed contract, I may have to raise your rates or decrease your feed allocation. I know you wouldn't want that to happen. If I don't do that, my superior will question me about giving the same favorable rates to a farm woman who has seen fit not to join the Farm Women's Group. Your children will find the positions they have worked hard to achieve in the Youth will be in danger if their mother has not been supportive enough of the state's policies to join the group of her peers. Do you see the extent of the damage you will do by failing to join?"

I saw after he spelled it out in such detail that there was no choice about joining the Farm Women's Group, it was in fact compulsory. So the following Saturday when I saw the woman at the market, I joined.

Of course, this was the beginning of other obligations that I had to incur as a member. I not only had to become a member, but I had to acquit myself as a good member. That entailed buying the newspaper when it was offered, even if I had already done so. It meant paying dues and paying them on time. I drew the line when the woman at the market suggested I might enjoy a cooking demonstration on how to provide a balanced diet for my family. I told her that I would be very eager to attend this demonstration, that I wanted desperately to learn how to provide such meals for my family, but that I would not be able to continue paying dues if I did not get back home at the usual time and keep the farm going. She duplicated my extreme politeness and told me that of course she understood that I wasn't organized to accommodate this interruption and that perhaps I would consider how to find time next month because this demonstration would be repeated. Perhaps, she suggested, I could hire someone to do the work I would miss by attending the demonstration. I told her that nothing would please me more and that I would make every effort so that my family would have the benefit of better nutrition.

It was getting harder to maintain the farm, not because the work was getting more difficult, but because demands on me were multiplying.

During this period Karl was preparing for a special contest organized by the Youth. He had devised an experimental project involving the chickens. There had been a sizable new batch of chicks hatched that January and Karl wanted to mark half the newborn chicks and give them cod liver oil drops once a week and see if more of them survived to laying age than the chicks that didn't get the oil. Naturally I had to perform this experiment since Karl had too many other obligations and I was around the chicks anyway. Karl was not particularly interested in the experiment itself, he just wanted to be able to enter the contest.

That year we had about thirty chicks born live and, using the India ink Karl had given me, I marked half of them on the web of the wing with an x. I gave these marked chicks the cod liver oil Karl gave me. For one thing, I had never put much stock in giving the chicks extra. Of course, before Nathanael we had always mixed our table scraps in with the feed for the chickens. Now, with Nathanael, we had no table scraps at all, except an occasional bone. Even the parts of things we had at one time thrown away, these we kept and used for soup. The result of the cod liver oil test was that at the end of six months, when the new chicks were ready to lay, we had eleven still living. When I checked the x marks I saw that just five of them were left. The others had been thinned out for one reason or another.

Karl was happy with the project, even though there was no conclusive result about the cod liver oil. When I asked him if he wanted to carry on giving the x-marked chicks the oil to see if it would improve their egg production, he said no. I told him I should get the prize for the contest, but that wasn't really so. I did the work so that Karl would not go into the chicken coop.

The market was always a source of gossip and a barometer of the mood of the village. Even I, who made no effort to be congenial, who may have given an impression either of aloofness or bad humor, got wind of the latest speculation that was making the rounds.

One day I came home from the market and went directly to the chicken coop without remembering to hum. Things I heard from the others had disturbed me.

"Nathanael, do you know what they're saying? I heard that a farmer with land he worked on the other side of the village was removed from his farm because he couldn't maintain the milk quota. Now have you ever heard of this? The Farm Bureau told him that he had to deliver so much and he persisted in keeping back some for butter and some to sell on the side and some for his own use, of course. There was one warning and then they took it away. He is now living in the city and plans to work in a factory. They say they did it as an example to the rest of us. To show us what will happen if we don't obey the Bureau supervisor. We would never survive if we lost this farm. What would happen to you?"

"It's getting closer every day, my Eva. You are like a hermit in your life. There is no way you can avoid it. You think it is only Jews? Only people who live in faraway cities? Only people who think about politics? This is now life as it is lived in this country. They may give a reason when they take this farm from you, but it will have nothing to do with you and you will not be able to stop them. You're lucky that people still need eggs."

"But if I can't get these chickens to lay enough? If they stop letting me sell at the market? If I lose the farm it would be like losing my family. All we know is farm work and farm life. You see how it is with you, you can barely keep your sanity here. The rhythm of my body, my brain and my muscles are those of a farm woman. It's not a hardship for me to draw the water fifty times a day. Generations of farm people can prepare the soil, sow seeds and wait for the rain. If it doesn't rain, we will do it again next year after a quiet grumble. Our life is with animals and growing things that we tend but cannot communicate with. We spend our time with things we cannot control, but we have become used to it. As babies we pet the pigs and then lick our fingers as the sausage juice dribbles down our chins. To us this all makes sense. We must keep this farm or lose our lives. My husband would never live down the shame of it."

At the mention of my husband Nathanael let go of my hand and stepped back. We never discussed my husband, though there were times I wanted to tell Nathanael what I felt. I knew he felt awkward at the thought that my husband might return. He felt that he had only a temporary place in my life story, a place that would be filled once again by my husband. I knew this was not true. Even though I expected my husband would return one day, I knew our life would never be as it was before. Even if Nathanael went out of my life, I could not imagine sleeping with my husband again. I did not want to discuss the eventuality of Nathanael leaving. We did not spend time speculating on the future.

SIX

One morning as I was pulling water from the well, I saw a woman from the market walking along the road. I was startled, since it was rare that anyone walked this road unless they were coming to visit our farm, or the one beyond. Though the road led to the village, there was a more convenient one, less likely to be flooded, that was a more direct route to the village. I recognized this woman because she was one of those who wandered the market chatting with everyone. She had the air of one who has to know all the gossip and sows a good part of it as she goes along her route. Words were easy for her, she had a way of striking up a talk without preliminaries and she never seemed to be at a loss for what to say.

There was little doubt in my mind that she was out for a visit with me. Although I did not show it, I was frightened of this woman; she could make gossip of my drawing water from the well, I thought.

"Good morning, my friend," she said, letting herself into the barnyard.

"Good morning to you," I replied, as heartily as I could manage. I was determined to be as accommodating as possible, though instinctively I was certain I should tell her only lies.

"Your children have left you to draw the water today, my friend?"

"I insisted they hurry off to school this morning after they did their chores. They do so much for me now that my husband is in the army. They do more than their share and then they want to draw the water besides. I told them I was more than capable of getting in the water and that I would get enough for their soup for the evening meal. Of course, they may not be home for the evening meal. So often they have extra work to do for the Youth, to prepare for a presentation or program. I know that the soup will be ready to heat up some time late tonight when they return. These children of today are so dedicated and busy." I startled myself with my effusion.

"Certainly, my friend, they are busy. And we are busy as well, are we not?"

"Naturally, we are, and pleasantly so. We're doing what little we can to maintain some semblance of normality while our husbands make sacrifices for our country. What we would do without them I don't really know."

"I agree with you entirely, my friend."

It occurred to me that this woman might have come for some free samples and I begged her to stay for a moment while I went into the chicken coop for some fresh eggs, hoping that there might be some. I hummed perhaps a little louder than usual as I made my way across the yard to the coop, went in and found half a dozen eggs, which I brought over to her in a basket. She demurred for a few minutes and then agreed to take them. She said she would return the basket to me at the market on Saturday. I thanked her and hoped she would like the eggs and would stay well until the next time we met. She thanked me for my wishes and said that she could not spare another moment and would absolutely have to leave. I asked her if she was sure she wouldn't like to sit with me and have a cup of tea and some biscuits, but she fortunately insisted she had to leave. We said our goodbyes again and I watched her go up the road toward the village.

When I saw this woman at the market, she returned to me the empty basket and showed me an invitation for a meeting of market vendors. I thanked her for showing it to me and tried to turn away. She asked me if I intended to attend the meeting. I said yes, I did. She said fine, she would see me there.

Of course, I had not even the smallest intention of attending any sort of meeting. I had no time and definitely no inclination to do so. On the market day after the meeting had taken place, this fiendish woman stopped at my stall in the square and told me how much she had looked forward to seeing me at the meeting and how she had looked among all those who had attended the most useful meeting, but had failed to find me among them. I acknowledged that I had been unable to attend, that I had set aside the time and remembered the meeting, looking forward to it since she had shown me the invitation, but at the last moment there had been a feed delivery and I had to stay in the barn mixing the mash for the chicks, and it had been totally impossible to let it go. I hoped that there would be another meeting in the near future that I could attend, so that I could learn how to improve my market practices. She said she could perfectly well understand how such an eventuality could interfere with one's plans at the last moment and that indeed there would be another meeting and I was more than welcome to attend if I could arrange the time, and she showed me another invitation and I said I would plan on attending. She told me she looked forward to seeing me there.

I knew this could not continue for long and I decided to get rid of this presence in my life by attending this particular meeting. I made the special trip back into the village and went to the school hall, where the meeting was scheduled to take place. I looked immediately for the fiendish woman so that she would be sure to see that I had attended. At first I didn't see her, but then, when the meeting was called to order, I noticed that she was at the front of the room with the three or four people facing the small audience. I went to one of the seats in the front rows and sat down. I nodded in recognition to a few of the vendors I noticed and they returned my nod, with some widening of their eyes to find me there. The subject of the meeting echoed the Blood and Soil theme that the state had been emphasizing for the past few years. I had never paid much attention to this slogan and what it might mean, either in general or to me in particular, but I was forced for the next hour to listen to the three speakers who had prepared their talks to us on this subject. The gist of it was that the farmers, all of us in the room, were the backbone of the country and it was our responsibility to carry on the pure blood of the country. Our blood was to carry on in our children and they were to continue this purity until there were only pure, unsullied human beings left. Likewise we were to provide for the rest of the country the food that would sustain them. We were too proud a country to depend on foreign producers to send us food or fodder for our animals, we could produce our own. We had already increased our self-sufficiency to nearly 80 percent and we would continue to do so until we never had to buy any essential commodity from any foreign country. Therefore we farmers held the rest of the country on our shoulders; we had their babies and we fed them.

This was quite a responsibility indeed. I left the meeting totally numb from hearing the same message from three different people, including the woman who had been to my farm. When I returned, I saw the children had not yet come home from their Youth activities, so I stopped by the chicken coop, even though it was not my practice to disturb the chickens at that hour, when they were already on the roost. I didn't hum as I entered, and they didn't come to greet me, but Nathanael did. His hands welcomed me into the darkness and we held each other close. His embrace was so comfortable for me, so familiar by now that it nurtured me with its warmth. I turned my face to him and told him something of what had been said at the meeting, then we lay together on his blanket.

"I am a bit stunned by what I heard this evening," I told Nathanael.

"You have been leading a sheltered existence, my Eva. You have been working so hard, drawing water, feeding animals, doing laundry, minding the weather, keeping up with things around here, that this philosophy has passed you by. Yet the nation is caught up with it. Everything is done by your blood. You have the right blood. I do not."

"Do you understand it, Nathanael?"

"Of course, I do. What a dolt I would be otherwise. I understand that I am not to be part of anything in this country. I cannot learn, I cannot buy, sell, make, work, do anything in this country. I am being asked, not so politely, to leave. I had the intention of doing just that when I took shelter in this chicken house. Perhaps it is time for me to continue on my interrupted way."

The conversation had taken a turn I did not want to follow, so I said nothing. We lay together for a short time without speaking and then I rose and went quietly into the house.

SEVEN

The most peaceful times for me were when the boy and his sister went on their weekend hikes into the mountains. I had less help but their help was so little in the first place that I didn't really miss it. They always gave priority to their Youth projects and when they had time they fitted in some of our farm work. On these weekends I felt I could perhaps spend more time with Nathanael who always welcomed my visits with caresses, kisses and lovemaking. We were able to talk a bit, just hold each other a bit, and take pleasure in each other. For the first time in my life I put off doing chores to pursue my own satisfactions.

The children always exuded great excitement when they returned from these weekend trips. They babbled gaily about things they had seen and what they had discussed. After one particular trip I had a shiver of excitement myself when my son described having seen the Swiss border from the top of a mountain he had climbed. Since childhood I had heard others speak of how near we were to this border, but it never had occurred to me that on foot one could reach it and in only days. I questioned my son and he told me where he had gone and how he had been able to continue on course with the help of a compass for direction. My son brought his compass from his room, showed it to me and explained the gist of how it worked. He was very proud of it and proud that he knew about something that I didn't. He explained all I needed to know in one breath: Switzerland is to our south and one has only to traverse the Black Forest to reach it; if one simply follows the compass and travels always south or southwest one will find Switzerland without fail.

"I wish you could see them, Mamma, the mountains, I mean. They are black indeed, black with trees where no light has ever penetrated, and if you look up, the trees are so tall that no ladder could reach their tops. If you try to walk through, you are stuck on all sides by a confusion of the lower branches of these trees interlocking into a barrier that will not let you pass. They are like a bramble obstacle course where you find another branch as soon as you turn from the one in front of you. It is a clever blockade of tree limbs. "Diabolical" our leader called them. You have to become a slithering snake and slide under them on your belly. Then you will find the roots of these incredible trees, themselves like snakes, thick as your arm, rising up out of the earth and crisscrossing over and under each other in a meshwork that prevents you from passing. It's as if the forest itself doesn't want to be breached. But, Mamma, the coolness of the forest is astounding. Even on this hottest of weekends, we had to put our extra sweaters on as soon as we entered the forest. It isn't just the temperature, which seems to drop at least twenty degrees at once, but it's a cathedral cold, a cold that is permanent, not ever to be warmed by anything, human or natural. But, Mamma, more than this, there was a presence in the forest, a black presence. It followed us everywhere we went until we reached the summit of the mountain from which we were able to see Switzerland. But in the forest, there was a definite presence, the presence of evil. It touched us all; it seemed to follow us as we walked. We all could feel it and we clung to each other even though we could not pass easily through the forest except one by one. But you'll be proud to know that after a night and a day, I, your son, acclimated myself even to this. I was able to feel at peace. Some of the others had to turn back because they were so petrified, they were unable to complete the hike. But, not I, your son. I was able to conquer even evil. Aren't you proud of me, Mamma?"

"Yes, of course, my son, that is remarkable, what you tell me. I would love to have this opportunity myself to see the things you have seen and done. You have experienced so much in your so short life."

"Mamma, as we lay on the ground, partly on the impossible twining roots, partly on layers of needles, so soft and so thick you felt there were centuries of needles under you, there was such a darkness, no light anywhere. Only the smell told us the pine trees were still there. The night was quiet, exaggeratedly quiet. I thought about Father somewhere, he too maybe sleeping in a forest with pine needles for a cushion. One day I will take his place in the army and he can come home to the farm. I think I was meant for his duty as he was meant for the farm."

The vision that my son described stayed with me for a long time afterwards. I imagined the tall trees and the scary forest, so lonely and mysterious. I asked my son if the group planned another trip into the forest.

"Yes, Mamma, we are to go again and see if we can find the trail we made the last time."

"What trail was that? How could there be a trail in the forest?"

"We made a trail ourselves with special markings on the trees so that we would be able to find our way back home again. Now we are supposed to find the trail and go over it again, perhaps extending it. We each brought with us a walking stick four-feet high and so, using it as a measure, we cut a small wedge out of each tree trunk at that height at intervals. Now when we go back, we merely have to look for the wedges in the trees. This should be a splendid trip.

"Mamma, did I tell you about the wind? I wonder if there will still be wind. In the dark, under the enormous trees that reach up in competition for the light, there is a constant noise of typhoon winds, winds that seem to have collected over the ages and cough and bellow into the trees. We, the brave forgers of paths in the woods, are struck dumb and while we hear the wind approaching from some distance, we can only stand in our tracks and look upwards, bracing ourselves for this mighty wind that must knock us to the ground with the force we can hear. But no, this wind does not trifle with us mere pinpoints of humanity. Standing there beneath these giant trees, we see the wind tossing the upper branches of the trees, assaulting the trees with violence, we imagine the caricature of the north wind with his cheeks puffed out, a pudgy cloud blowing with all his might against the insignificant trees. There we were, standing transfixed watching, it seemed, the wind pass over us, challenging the trees with a taste of the power that might be unleashed to its maximum against them. I wrote a story for our Youth magazine about this. The story tells how we will be as strong and resistant as the trees, especially when we are massed all together as they are in a forest, all supporting each other against the evil wind."

"Why, you surprise me with this story. I will certainly be most interested to see it, my son."

"Thank you, Mamma."

I thought about my son making this path across the mountains. Leaving marks on trees so that someone else could find the path after him. My son was going to lead Nathanael to safety. But when? It had been understood all along that one day Nathanael would be leaving. Here he was in constant peril and so were we. One could live in a chicken coop only so long. There was no question one day it would have to end.

EIGHT

As I think about those years I see my limitations. I was still learning how to be tender. I see I was a woman whose head was bowed over her work and her life, without a sign of self pity. She did not dream for more or something different. This farm woman was a stranger to herself as much as to those around her. She worked and slept, and nothing more. She did not imagine doing less work, had no thought of rebellion or complaint. To complain would imply that there was an alternative. For this woman there was none. She has something pathetic about her, the sense that she feels herself to be fortunate to be drudging through her life this way. She doesn't feel overworked, at least not unfairly so.

I am looking at her, that is my older, that is my younger, self, crossing the barnyard a thousand times a day, doing the same chores every day as if propelled by the passing of the sun across the sky, rather than in reaction to human urges. The me that was she was not seeking something I might now call happiness. She was surviving. Her parents, my parents, were assuring my survival when they found me my husband, dispensing with a worry, or rather passing it along to him. I felt that I had to do my share in alleviating other people's responsibility for me. At some point I looked at this woman, so many years spent paying off her debt for existing, as if in slavery to the world into which she had been apologetically born, never buying freedom with her labor, only the continued permission to exist. This was not tragic for her, it was normal. Nature itself has provided the work for her to do, not an alien taskmaster. The weeds have grown, the cows need milking, the chickens must be fed, the children require tending, all these things evolving out of their natural healthy state. On the trips to the well there is no thought that the water might be available in pipes, leading the horses through the fields, there is no idea that a tractor might simplify the tedious and difficult job of plowing. These advances are not part of her life. They were devised for some fortunate folk, but she never considered herself in that category. As I think about her pride in each day's payment to the world for another day's sufferance, I understand the shell she was. Inside there was nothing, nothing particularly human. There was no initiative, nothing began with a thought, a desire, a wish. Everything she did was for the upkeep of the farm, not according to someone's opinion, but according to nature, according to necessity. The pigs are fed, if they are not fed they make an enormous noise, like cows that need to be milked or chickens that haven't been fed and watered. This farmer's wife did not wonder if it was time to feed the pigs; there was nothing to wonder about. But neither did she wonder about whether she was meant to lead this particular life with this particular routine. On a farm, this was the only routine there was, by nature. There was no habit of having choices, of making decisions, of evaluating and judging the difference between options.

A different woman emerged, one might almost say a woman stepped from the silhouette of a farmer's wife. This woman had thoughts and desires and wishes. This was the difference. It was not even immediately obvious, but I knew it as it was happening. I felt that my thoughts, previously simply recordings of what needed doing next, were taking form like dialogues in my head. As I did various chores, as I drew the water, as I prepared the vegetables for our stew, I discussed things with myself. I thought about Nathanael. I questioned myself. When it occurred to me that concealing Nathanael in the chicken coop was a decision that I had failed to make, that I had just let it happen, I concluded that it was what I wanted. Now it was approaching a year and a half that Nathanael was living in the chicken coop. I realized that I had the power to determine whether or not he remained. Slowly my under-standing became more concrete and what it meant became clear. I could ask Nathanael to leave and let his fate rest elsewhere. The exhilaration that I felt when I understood this stayed with me a long time.

I was becoming somewhat detached. I continued to carry out all my chores, go to the market every week, deliver the eggs every other day, take care of the house and the meals, feed the chickens and do the work of the farm. There was perhaps something more, something additional. I was concentrating on something, going through the motions of my usual routine, but thinking of something else, the way one does before Christmas, thinking about it, even though one is busy with other things, until the time arrives. All the while one is thinking of the special foods to be made, tablecloths to be readied, presents collected, at the same time one continues the regular routine. I took great pleasure in my time with Nathanael. Our relationship was something I didn't think about ending, either by my own initiative or because of outside events. For me our time together was a necessary element of the day, had become part of my routine.

Thoughts of my husband were provoked by his occasional letters to remind me of various things that would need doing. There were long stretches when he sent no word at all. His letters were short and reflected his concern that the farm not be abandoned while he was gone. I knew the embarrassment he felt at asking one of his soldier friends to write for him, so I answered only when it seemed essential and then only letters he would not mind having a stranger read.

I got into the habit of talking some things over with Nathanael, even though he knew nothing of farming. He was intelligent and the act of describing a problem and the various possible solutions often clarified things for me. If I could set out the situation clearly for Nathanael, likely I could solve the problem. Nathanael helped during the winter egg hatching when the tiny chicks needed special attention. Probably his presence in the coop ensured our ability to augment the flock for the following season, pulling us out of the low egg numbers we had experienced. I told Nathanael how the convent was in such difficulties and how I tried to help out. Nathanael was interested, as he always was in the things I told him about the outside world. Usually he didn't comment on what I told him; he knew I was only making conversation, not expecting his advice or hoping to keep him informed. Actually I was his only form of diversion, I was the only person he spoke with, the only one he saw. I noticed his eagerness for my visits and the enjoyment he derived even when I passed along the gossip from the marketplace. I told him what the other vendors said, how the woman bothered me about the meetings, the prices I got for my eggs, and he never made any comment about it. If I sounded content, he seemed to be as well. Nathanael never asked me questions about what was going on, what anyone in particular was saying. He didn't press me for details or make inquiries. I didn't tell him about my son's path over the mountains. I told him everything else.

It wasn't only with respect to Nathanael that this woman was emerging. I was dealing with the other vendors in the marketplace, my customers, the Farm Bureau man and frequent decisions regarding the chickens and other animals. There was the question of the convent. My relationship with the convent had continued along the same lines as originally. Sister Karoline would send me the box with the money inside and occasionally a new order and I would send it back with the eggs inside. The orders were continually increased. From two dozen, the sisters were consuming five or six dozen eggs a week. At this period we heard there was a shortage of eggs in the cities and in fact there were new faces at the market each week, looking not for bargains but for supplies. These new faces were willing to buy anything. They said very little, accepting the first price they were told, and they bought more than you thought they could use. One week no one came from the convent to deliver the box, which by then was three boxes, and I had set aside the usual order of five dozen eggs. When I had sold off everything but the five dozen, two live birds and all the eggs, even the slightly cracked ones, I walked over to the convent and pulled the bell. A tiny sister opened the door and quickly closed it. I waited and rang again and finally Sister Karoline came bustling out to meet me at the gate. Rather than invite me in, she wiped her flour-covered hands on a towel hanging from her belt and asked me why I had come.

"Why, Sister, it has been nearly a year now that every single week you have ordered eggs from me, more and more each month. Today you give me no warning and no one comes for the eggs. I thought you might have forgotten."

"Dear Egg Woman, how could you be expected to have known. We are in deep trouble here at the convent and no one has given a thought to our provisions. The burden of our differences with the state has affected us deeply. We cannot accept the policy on sterilization, we deplore the decline in marriages, we feel laws have been directed against ourselves. We are not being permitted to sell our land now. We have been forbidden to run our schools. Why? Because we will not swear to our leader over our savior. Our own superiors have ordered us to maintain our faith. If the state does not respect us, we will have to accept our punishment. There is more, but how can I tax you with our many troubles. Please wait here and I will fetch the egg money."

Her recitation was disturbing to me, but I did not really think any of these was the real reason for her failing to continue her egg-ordering routine. I suspected something else was going on, but why, I didn't know myself. As I stood at the gate waiting, a somewhat embarrassing position, not having been asked in even as far as the entryway, I looked at the windows of the convent. I saw the little sister who had opened the door for me and saw her racing from room to room. Then I realized that these little ones could be seen at every window, and several at some. Those little figures in black shrouds scampering before the windows were eerie. Where could they have found so many new sisters, and no one ever mentioned them. Possibly these were the children the sisters took care of. Maybe they had something to do with how many eggs the convent ordered. Of course they would need more eggs if they had all these extra people to feed.

When Sister returned with the money, I gave her the eggs I had brought and asked her if she would need any for the next week. She said she would and did I have an extra chicken or two also. I told her I would save two for her if I had them. I suggested she might want me to bring the eggs and chickens to the convent direct and she agreed.

NINE

One morning I was unable to get out of bed. I raised up my head and tried to move my legs over the side of the bed to the floor. My legs wouldn't move at all and my head swirled wildly. I tried to call out to get some help, but my voice wouldn't come. Finally my daughter came to the door of my bedroom and asked me if something was wrong; it was past time of rising and tending the cows and chickens. I tried to answer, but couldn't. She came to my bedside and asked me what was wrong, and seeing me trying to raise my head, came to help me sit up in the bed. I still couldn't move my legs and didn't think I could talk.

"Mamma, please say something, you look horrible. You are completely white and your eyes look funny. What's wrong with you?"

"I...Aiy...yii...aiee..." I just couldn't form the sounds, but I didn't know what was wrong.

"Karl, come quickly, Mamma's sick, Mamma can't talk. Karl, come here in Mamma's bedroom, Mamma is sick."

"Why, Mamma, what's the matter? I have never known you to be sick before this. What do you feel? Shall I call the doctor?"

"No, Karl," my daughter said, "we aren't calling any doctor. Remember that story about the people who called the doctor and even though the doctor wasn't able to do anything he announced some terrible diagnosis and they took the farm away because the person was sick."

"Don't exaggerate this, Olga. Mamma, surely will feel better after having some breakfast. Right, Mamma? We'll get you some breakfast and we'll bring it right to you and you'll feel ever so much better. Now let me fetch a pillow to put behind you here and you will sit quietly until we come back with your breakfast."

The way my son took charge was somewhat surprising to me, I was proud that he could seem to take control that way. Of course, what my daughter had said was very true. I had heard stories in the village of similar incidents where the doctor, not knowing the reason for someone's illness caused them to be marked down with some disease, like spells or fits, that would have the farm withdrawn from them. The village people seemed to think the doctors were incompetent since the new laws had come into effect and their lack of experience and expertise forced them to invent a diagnosis. I sat in the bed with my head feeling like a giant cabbage that I was having trouble balancing on my neck. It was rolling around, never finding a place of repose and equilibrium. When they came upstairs with the coffee and bread I took one look and vomited on the tray, after an instinctive move to spare the bedclothes. The children were completely appalled, as was I. Karl disposed of the tray and Olga brought me some water, which I managed to swallow in the smallest sips. As often happens, within minutes I felt better. I returned almost immediately to my usual self and without difficulty swung my legs over the side of the bed onto the floor and stood up. My dizziness had completely left me and I found my voice had returned and my senses. I thanked the children for their care, for getting the breakfast, even though I hadn't been able to eat it, and told them to get along to school that I felt fine and would be able to continue along with the day as usual. They were somewhat skeptical, but seeing that I was already on my feet and beginning to get dressed, they left me and went downstairs.

Later that day, standing in the barn after cleaning the stalls, I realized what it was that had caused my strange illness that morning. I was pregnant. I was pregnant with Nathanael's baby, and my baby. Growing within me was Nathanael's and my baby. I felt a surge of joy. Followed by a cold chill.

I allowed myself to be alone with our baby for a few days. That is, I didn't tell Nathanael immediately about it. I wondered whether I should tell him at all, and when. I was quite transported with the presence of the baby. It had been so long ago that my two babies had been born, I had forgotten the feeling. I could feel the baby's sex, a boy. I felt his particularity, knew him as himself, not an abstract something in my body. I thought about the future, the baby's future, in confusion. Would Nathanael be still there in the chicken coop? Was the father of my baby, our baby, to be an outcast from all society, hiding for eternity? Was this what the future held for this baby? I could think only of the present continuing on forever. I knew that could not be, but I was reluctant to acknowledge it since I feared what might replace it. I was content for now. I was little troubled by what my husband might say, finding a baby after having been so long away. I could not contemplate my husband returning to the farm. Our tradition is to imagine the future to be better than the present, that one's children will find a life always more rich, more easy than our own. I could not see such a future for my children or anything better on the horizon for this baby. I imagined with horror that this little child might join the national adventure, despite who his parents were.

I wanted this baby very much. It was special for me that the baby was Nathanael's. Over the months Nathanael had taken shelter in the chicken coop, he had been a source of many new things for me. He treated me with respect. He tried to give to me, not just demand. In fact he never asked me for anything. If I was unable to bring him food for one reason or another, as happened several times when there was a visitor, or when I was detained in the village, he never mentioned it. He never expressed dislike for anything I gave him or did for him. When I smuggled him into the house periodically for a bath, he was delighted, but he never requested it. Nathanael tried to please me. Because of his dependency on me, he wanted to make me happy. I saw him watch my reaction to things he did. When we were together lying on his blanket, holding each other, he often asked me if there was something I liked him to do, and I always did. He was the first person who ever considered if I was comfortable, tired, happy or sad. Even my own mother had been too busy with the other children and her chores to worry about if one of us needed something. We only got special attention when we were sick, and that was so that we shouldn't pass it on to everyone else.

For an instant it occurred to me that I might be able to keep Nathanael near me if we had this baby to watch. As though the baby would have the power to keep us together. Only for an instant. The habit of practicality was too strong in me to sustain such an irrational thought. Nathanael would not be a permanent part of my life. He was only passing through, even though it was more than a year since he had come to the farm. Was he going to leave behind this baby for me?

When I approached Sister Karoline the following Saturday, she was so nervous that she could keep no part of herself still. She circled around me, touched my shoulder a few times, retreated to the door and returned. I heard some soft noises in the background, footsteps shuffling on the stone floors, down corridors, up stairs. I had the feeling Sister wanted to ask me something or tell me something, but when I suggested she might want to increase her order, maybe she would need more or fewer chickens the following week, or several other changes, to each one she said, "No, no, no, my child, nothing of the kind." I gave up trying to guess her difficulty, and just waited. Shortly she came out with it. "My dear Egg Woman, I was wondering..."

"Yes, Sister," I encouraged.

"Well, how to say? I thought to myself, how hard the Egg Woman must work. Feeding chickens, collecting eggs, drawing water, all the rest. Life on your farm must be hard. Your husband had gone to the army, isn't it so?"

"Yes, Sister, he has," I answered.

"How many workers have you taken for the season, Egg Woman?"

"Why, Sister, we do not have workers on our farm. It's quite small, really. I have two children who give me some help."

"But can that be enough? Surely your children, willing though they may be, have responsibilities with the Youth."

"Yes, they do, Sister."

"Then probably you will be needing some help for the coming season."

The tone with which Sister spoke those words was not in her usual gentle, rather preoccupied manner. She was disguising an order, one that was difficult to ignore, as an idle suggestion. Sister was telling me she needed me to do something for her and she was looking for an excuse we could agree on.

"It sounds to me, Sister, that you are in need of some help. Would you like to tell me about it?"

"No, my child, I would not, but in these days of pain and anguish, I find that I must implicate more and more people in fulfilling God's work. We have tried to do what we could alone but the need is so great that it is no longer possible. Can you understand me?"

"Sister, you are talking in hidden language to me, but it would be better if you simply told me what you need and I will tell you if I can provide it for you. You needn't worry that I will betray you to some authorities. We have been fighting the authorities for years and still they force us to pretend that we are complying with everything they require. If I had followed all the regulations we would be starving on our farm, without butter, milk and proper feed for the chickens. But you don't want to discuss farm policy with me. What exactly do you want from me, Sister?"

"I have staying here in the convent a young girl who needs a place to stay. She wants to work on a farm. Do you have a place for her?"

"She would want to live at the farm?"

"Yes, that would be best."

"She would work?"

"Dear Egg Woman, I will tell you now, she has no experience whatever in farm work. She knows nothing about it. She comes from a city, rather far away. She needs our help. Can you do it?"

I was unprepared for this suggestion and my first thought was that it would imperil Nathanael to bring someone to live on the farm. I attempted to provide an escape hatch that would not endanger my good relations with Sister Karoline. She had pre-empted me in requesting this favor, as I had been preparing to ask one of her when she began her roundabout presentation.

"Do you think we might try it out for a month or so? How about if we give it a chance and leave it open for her and for me that if we prefer to cancel the arrangement we can do it easily."

Sister Karoline grabbed the unenthusiastic offer.

"I think we can agree to that. You will find her very willing, very anxious to please you. I can have her ready in a moment."

With that Sister swept into the convent and within less than five minutes was back dragging a somewhat reluctant little child, who in turn was dragging a shawl-wrapped package behind her. This frail little person looked about seven years old. I was shocked and looked at Sister with widened eyes and a questioning look, which she ignored. Obviously she had planned this exchange and had the child ready and waiting for me to deliver the eggs.

"Thank you so much, my dear Egg Woman. We hope that you and Mary will have a nice day. I'll see you next week."

With that Sister gathered up her robes, turned on her heel and went inside and closed the door as we, Mary and I, stood on the step.

I began to babble a bit, out of my own nervousness and the second thoughts that had been slammed shut with the door. "Well, I guess we had better be on our way home. You don't know the way, but here, you carry this box and I'll carry the rest and we will be there in no time. So how are you, Mary?"

She didn't answer.

"Mary, do you want to answer me?"

Nothing.

"Well, Mary, lots of people don't talk very much, that's not to be ashamed of. Do say something, just so that I know you can talk if you wanted to."

Nothing.

"Hmmm. I see. You would rather not. Well, I could have a conversation, both asking questions and answering them too, but I think I'll wait until we get home." So we made the entire trip back to the farm with not one sound from Mary. I felt that Mary was not so much antagonistic as frightened. She didn't know how I might react to what she said and feared displeasing me so she said nothing at all. Much safer. As we walked along I saw that Mary was stealing little glances at me to take my measure. She had to evaluate how much she might trust me to be kind. I carried on down the road as though she wasn't there and she just kept up with me, falling a few steps behind and catching up with a skip.

When we got to the farm, I told Mary she would have to sleep in my bed and I showed her around the farm, explaining carefully that no one ever went into the chicken coop but me. I showed her how to draw water, how to do all the things that needed to be done on the farm. When the time came, as it shortly did, to prepare dinner, I sat Mary down with an apronful of peas and two pots, one for the peas, one for the pods. I showed her what needed doing and left her alone. When I returned I saw that there was only a smallish amount of peas and a large pile of pods. I was infuriated. "How dare you eat up our peas? You've stolen the food from our mouths. What could have possessed you to do a thing like that?" The answer to my question, screamed out of surprise and betrayal, was only too clear. Mary was famished.

Mary was looking at me with total confusion and dismay on her slight little face as it tilted toward me quizzically. "Oh, Mary, didn't they feed you at the convent?"

She refused to answer me at all. I had taken this at first for shyness, insecurity, not out of place in this circumstance. Now I didn't see shyness, I saw that she was not defiant, not feeling guilty at what I thought to be a rather grave offense. Mary had done what for her was the natural thing. She had been deprived for so long that it never occurred to her that the peas would be part of a larger meal shared by us all. She simply had taken advantage of an opportunity to quiet her perpetual hunger. She was perplexed at my reaction. I was not going further until she answered me.

"Mary, do you understand my words?"

She nodded.

"Do you know that you have done a bad thing in eating all, or almost all, our peas?"

She shook her head.

"Can you explain, please, why you are not answering me with words? We cannot continue this way. If you don't answer me I will have to send you back to Sister Karoline." Evidently that did it, for Mary said, "No."

"Are you hungry, Mary?"

"No."

"Then why have you eaten all the peas?"

She just shrugged her shoulders.

"Mary, will you talk to me?"

"No."

I told her to go into the house. I wanted to consult with Nathanael, who I knew was watching everything and listening from the chicken coop window.

When I came into the coop Nathanael said, "Where have you found this little item?"

"Actually she's from the convent. Sister Karoline asked me to take care of her. She said she would work for me."

"She ate all the peas, of course. You have taken on a new, very hungry burden, my Eva."

"How so?"

"This little girl is probably a Jewish orphan, or passing for an orphan, but her parents are submarines for the moment. They have gone underground or have taken on other identities. They think Mary is safe now in the convent, and they plan to come back for her some day when there is no danger. She was given protection in the convent, but now they may have too many and have to place the children elsewhere, because they don't have enough food or the Gestapo has become suspicious or threatening. Do you not notice your little girl is so dark and pinched?"

"The convent is protecting Jewish children?"

"It has been doing so for some years now. The parents decide that things have become too hot, either they think they're about to be arrested or they plan to take on some dangerous activity and they give their children away. They think it's only temporary, but they want to protect their children in this way."

"But are these children being given the teachings of the Church?"

"Who knows? The Church is in such chaos at the moment that it can't provide teaching for its own. The children in the public schools are taught to pray to the leader. The church schools have been disbanded. The churches will be closed before long, but even if they remain, no one can attend them. They have put photographs of the leader above the paintings of Jesus. This is a new religion."

"Poor Mary."

"That can't be her real name. She may not even remember it. They must have dozens of Marys and Josephs now in the convent. So you now have me and Mary to take care of. You will have to talk fast when the Farm supervisor comes. Eva, you are getting in more deeply than ever."

"But what shall I say to our Mary? She won't talk to me. Did you hear?"

"Probably she doesn't want you to notice her city accent. Maybe Sister or her mother told her not to talk so that people wouldn't suspect that she came from the city."

"We will manage with Mary."

"May I give such a remarkable person a kiss?"

My motives were not so pure that I should be rewarded. If I sent Mary, or whatever her name was, away, wouldn't I be that much closer to being able to send Nathanael away. With Nathanael there was no longer a question of it. Now this Mary, such a small child, how could one send her away? What was it about her that was Jewish? Now she was only the second Jewish person I had met and she and the other were both living on this farm and under my protection.

TEN

The following week when I returned to the convent for the delivery, I knew I had to raise the subject I had been ready to raise the previous week. Only this time, Sister was in my debt. She had exposed herself and her entire order to my trust and now we were both in danger and mutually in debt in a certain way. Sister opened the door and quickly came out to the gate to speak to me. She took the eggs and two chickens and asked how Mary was getting along.

"Mary's fine, Sister, but I wonder if you could give me the name of a doctor nearby whom I might trust."

"Well, we have a doctor living here in the convent with us. May I ask what the problem is so that I can talk to her about it and let you know next week."

"I would prefer not to divulge the nature of the problem, nor whom it concerns. I would like to speak directly with the doctor if it is possible."

"Please wait here, dear Egg Woman, I will see if she's free."

Shortly afterward Sister Karoline returned with a very small woman, about forty years old. I glanced toward Sister, who I could see was interested in hearing the details, and murmured to the doctor that I would like to speak with her privately.

"What can I help you with, my dear?" she said when we had walked a few steps away.

"I find I am to have a baby."

"I see. And what do you wish from me?"

"I have decided that I cannot have this baby. I want to save this baby."

"Save the baby. Well, I think I understand you. You want to spare the baby this life, is that it?"

I nodded.

"Next week when you come to the convent to deliver your eggs, please remember not to eat anything for one day before. Ring the bell as you usually do and tell Sister you have a present for the doctor."

With those words she turned and went into the convent. Sister was still waiting by the door and after the doctor went inside, she waved to me and I waved back and walked away.

I thought over the doctor's words about what was going to take place. I was frightened, but quite certain that I was going to do the right thing. I had not doubted what I should do, I didn't weigh two choices. For me there was either a dream world or reality and I knew which was which. My sense of living in the present was so strong that it ruled out acting according to fantasy. To protect the child within me I had to liberate it from the life we had.

Meanwhile, Mary concerned us very much. Both the children were angry with me when they came home and found her there. They asked me how much she would cost to keep and why couldn't I continue to handle the farm work as we had been doing. I didn't give their arguments much weight and was only polite in responding to them. The things that concerned me were larger and larger all the time. Nathanael, of course, now myself, now Mary, not to mention pleasing the Farm Bureau supervisor on his monthly inspections, continuing to take care of the chickens, the regular farm upkeep, my husband's long-distance demands and the children's daily needs.

Mary was a distraction from all the other thoughts. My attitude with her was firm, very firm, but essentially gentle. I was immensely curious about her. Was Nathanael right about why she was in the convent? She must have felt very alone in such a place. The sisters, kind as they were, could hardly replace her mother or family. She had been old enough to know that she had been intentionally abandoned by her parents. Even though they must have explained everything to her, if they had had the time, Mary was probably too young to understand anything other than that her parents were sending her away. This thought made me more tolerant of the moody, uncommunicative little child we had taken possession of. I told my children to be especially considerate of Mary since she had lost her parents, taking advantage of the double meaning of the word. Even when I explained how I had been asked to take her by the Sister, the children did not accept Mary as deserving of being in our house. I also stressed that Mary would be an additional hand on the farm, at which they became hysterical at the idea that this tiny little thing could even haul a pail of water from the well. I insisted they be polite to Mary and they maintained the minimum acceptable.

On the following Saturday I followed my usual market day routine. I was tense, to be sure, but I concentrated on setting aside what it was that bothered me. I packed the eggs and picked up the only chicken I needed and walked to the village. After I had sold most of the eggs at the square, I went to the convent and, after giving her the egg order, told Sister Karoline that I had a present for the doctor. She wasted no time in shooing me inside the door, eager to close it behind me, and calling for the doctor. As I looked around the anteroom I found myself in, my reason for being there took hold of me with a shudder. I had successfully avoided thinking about this appointment for the whole week, fearing my own weakness. The doctor, small as she was, projected strength and competence as soon as she appeared. She was confident and strong, and took me by the arm with hers like a longtime friend and walked me to the stairs. It was as I had seen others do as I sat in the square selling eggs every week. Two well-dressed young women would come into the square arm in arm and turn toward each other completely engrossed in describing something. Their heads would be almost touching, their hair neatly pulled back off a lovely forehead and gathered at the back of the neck. First one, then the other would listen and then add a thought, then listen again until eventually they would either both laugh or both nod in agreement. This was how it felt to go slowly up the stairs with the doctor, arm in arm, she speaking softly to me all the time, but not expecting me to answer. It seemed that this had been the reason for my visit, so unhurried and relaxed was she.

"Egg Woman, you must have spent a very uncomfortable week since we last met. I have been thinking about you every day. I admire you very much for what you are doing today. You are a strong woman with a strong mind. May I tell you something about myself so that you will know with whom you are sharing this quite special day? I won't bother you with my name, but if you go to the capital you will find in the central hospital there everyone knows me very well.

I imagine they will try to separate the doctor I am from the woman I am, but of course they err. As a doctor, they may say, she had no peer. She was at the head of the class in medical school, she worked harder than anyone else, she was determined to become a doctor, even though few had succeeded before her. But she, they will be referring to me, stayed in the laboratory later than anyone else and did more research and more experiments than the other students and led the life of a hermit in order to succeed. Well, speaking of me as a doctor they will be forced to concede that I was superior on every score. I was able to elicit the most minute details from a patient in order to make a proper diagnosis, I could explain in simple language the procedures we intended to perform, I had the loyalty of the nursing staff and their respect, given grudgingly to only a few. I took myself seriously as a doctor and although it was plain from my first year that medical knowledge has advanced only a few steps from a primitive tribal shaman or medicine man, I decided that I would dedicate myself to helping people fight their illnesses, with me as their primary weapon. For many years I was able to be at the side of patients who came to me with weaknesses and worries and after a while left knowing we had together done what we could to beat down the illness.

"As a doctor, my colleagues at the hospital could not find a word of criticism against me. We worked together with only minor jealousies interrupting a very stimulating relationship. They came to consult with me regarding their most difficult cases and in turn I had them read some of my insoluble ones. Perhaps you know the way the system works. Each doctor belongs to the Medical Association and the state reimburses the hospital and the doctor for the expenses of the patients. Some years ago new eligibility rules were established for membership in the Medical Association. At first no one paid any attention. We all continued on as before. Then one of the newer doctors on the staff realized that if there was an opening he could receive a promotion. There were no openings. Soon I received a notice that informed me I would no longer be eligible to belong to the Medical Association. I charged into the director's office and showed him the notice.

"'Can you imagine receiving such a communication, sir?' I asked him. 'I have been advised that I cannot belong to the association. That would mean I would have to leave the hospital. It would mean I couldn't practice medicine at all, in effect.'

"'I read it that way too, my dear. What can we do? We don't make the rules. If you continue here, we will be sent to concentration camps for re-education. We will be punished for keeping you and you will still be out of a job.'

"'Does this not go further than just being out of a job?' I asked the director.

"He looked at me sadly. By that time in my life I knew not to expect people to commit suicide for you. Who is the one who will say, 'Fire me too, for if you fire her unjustly, I won't work here.' What purpose will that serve, you know? So two are out of work, one unjustly and one stupidly, one for hate and one for love. Not good enough.

"If you go back to the hospital now to ask about me, they will speak only ill. They will be afraid to say anything good about me as a doctor, afraid to praise a non-person, so they will discuss me only as a person. They will tell you that I belong to those who would take over the country from its rightful citizens. They will tell you that I was taking the place of a more worthy soul, me a woman and a Jew. They will tell you that I tried to push ahead of everyone else, people more deserving than I of honors and prestige. They, who one day knew I was superior to them as doctors, will declaim how I am inferior to them in a more basic genetic sense. They will tell you that while they used to say I should have been at home having babies all the time I was spending studying and excelling, now I am not even worthy of having babies at all. That my babies are not worthy of life."

All the while she spoke softly and simply to me, her head as close to mine as our discrepancy in height would allow, as we slowly climbed the stairs to one of the uppermost floors of the convent. My eyes were fixed on her face as she told me these things about herself. Her voice was lovely, melodic and clear and she did not need to raise it to be heard easily. I watched as she spoke: her eyes were cold, her only hint of emotion; her eyes were hard; I saw in her eyes that she could do anything. But her voice was as lilting as if she were telling me a child's tale of fantasy. She dramatized her story with various inflections and different voices. We stopped at one of the doors and we went in together. She never left me for a moment. She helped me out of my clothes, gently and slowly, betraying no haste or curiosity, as if she had always done so and would again tomorrow. All the while she continued to speak to me. She gave me a wrap to put on and showed me how to tie the waist up, taking an extra minute to evaluate the bow she had made with her head tilted to one side. We sat down on a soft chair that was big enough for both of us and she put her arm around me and asked me only two questions, how far along I was and how I was feeling. She nodded at my answers and guided me towards a shelf in one part of the room where she combined some water with some powder and gave it to me to drink. She stood with me as I swallowed the mixture and while she didn't explain what it was, I had no reluctance whatever in drinking it down. Then she pulled out from next to the wall a cot with a mattress covered with clean white sheets, where she helped me to lie down. She placed something under the mattress so that it raised up under my knees and gave me a pillow for under my head. All the while she continued to talk to me in her beautiful, tuneful voice.

"Sister Karoline mentioned that Mary has gone to live with you. I'm sure that you are curious about what Mary is doing going to work on a farm. Surely she doesn't know one thing about farming, she has never done work in her little life. Mary looks like nine or ten years old, but in reality she is at least fifteen. She has been deprived of so many things that she has stopped growing completely. Some of her teeth have fallen out but new ones will not replace them. She has never had her menstrual period and may never have it. She has been in a continual state of hunger for many years. She has become used to lying and sneaking and living in hiding. She cannot remember having had a real life, she hasn't been to school in years, she has forgotten any learning she may have known. Experience has taught her to withhold her trust entirely, from everyone, without distinction, without exception. She is not sick, by the way, I have examined her, as I have all the children, and Mary is free of disease. She has suffered permanent damage in terms of her physical growth, yes, but she will live.

"From many points of view it would be interesting to follow Mary's mental condition for a few years. If times return to normal, will Mary also return to normal? This I do not know. For Mary right now it is better to be as she is. For Mary normal meant having a family, sisters and brothers and a happy household. Her mother was a nurse and her father a storekeeper. They were not rich people, but they never wanted for anything, and they had more than most. Nurses have always been in demand and the store had been in the family for generations and was not encumbered with debts. Mary's family was strong and thriving. I said happy, right? They were happy. First you will remember that the new rules forbid anyone to buy from Jews. I have taken for granted that you knew Mary is Jewish, dear Egg Woman. You did know that, didn't you? Well, she is. And when the rules came down that no one could patronize a store owned by Jews, Mary's father found all his loyal customers went an extra block or two out of their way to give their business to the storekeeper sanctioned by the authorities. For a while Mary's mother kept her job at the hospital, there being a shortage always of nurses of her caliber. Mary's father, meanwhile, having so much time on his hands, was contacted by the underground, the opposition, you know, the so-called troublemakers. By now he had sold his inventory to his competitor down the block, closed the store and spent his days watching over the children with his mother-in-law, driving his wife to work and picking her up every day. He was approached by the underground and asked to help them transport some children to the countryside. There was no good reason not to help some children in this way, so Mary's father began driving back and forth between the capital and this village taking children to the convent in his car. Today we have thirty children staying with us. Thirty beautiful children whose parents were in peril and thought only, even as you do, of saving their children. These children now living in the convent, as well as those we have managed to place around the countryside, like Mary with you, may never see their parents again. We know that. They do not know it. Probably their parents, if they still breathe, know it. They have made the most beautiful sacrifice. They have twice given their children life. They knew what lay ahead for themselves and they sent their children to the future. As you are doing.

"Mary's father made many trips to the convent until on his last trip he had Mary with him with a little suitcase, just like the other little children had with them. He rang the bell, as always, a dignified gentleman, who could not get out of the habit of treating everyone he met with the deference he had always paid his customers. He rang the bell and Sister answered as usual, she always answers the bell, despite the many other responsibilities she carries. He greeted Sister in his usual unhurried way, as though he would be pleased to show her his entire stock three times over if she so desired. She, not so patient in these days as she tells me she used to be, greets him and prepares to accept the child he has with him. Mary's father holds her hand, she with her eyes lowered to the ground, and tells Sister that this is his daughter Rebecca and that he would be pleased and she would be grateful if Sister would be able to find a place for Rebecca to stay for a while, until he and his wife can come to take their daughter home again. Sister, usually so tactful even though she can be brusque, was overpowered by the poignancy of the situation. She is embarrassed, her defenses, so carefully constructed, are shaken, and rather than allowing her pain to show, Sister grabs Rebecca's hand out of her father's and says, 'Sure. Come along, now, let's go inside.' I'm sure Sister's instincts were right. I told her she had done them both a favor. Long farewells are poisonous and last well beyond their deserved length. I told her that in the future they would be grateful that she had not allowed them time to add to the pain they would be spending their lives trying to dissolve. Sister has since then had a special feeling of having to make amends to Mary, as she was immediately told she would be called. Sister from the first gave Mary every comfort and every consideration, allowed her to have more frequent baths, extra portions of food and fewer chores. Even though she had never known any of the other children's parents, her poor handling of Mary's arrival at the convent blotted out everything else for her. That's why she decided to find a better place for Mary as soon as we got word that our sanctuary would not last too much longer.

"I spent some time with Mary, who was in fact sort of shell-shocked, traumatized from that first moment. Whether it was Sister's doing or not, I don't know. But Mary told me that her father explained that his work driving for the underground had put him and her mother on the arrest list and he had been warned to prepare. Her parents had taken advantage of this convent as a refuge for Mary, the only place they knew of. Mary understands—at least, with her reason she does.

"Well, what to do? Who are we to judge Mary's parents and the parents of all these children with us and in other parts. I too have joined them in exile."

As she spoke to me, mesmerizing me, shocking me with her story, she massaged me, beginning with my arms, gently stroking my forearms until they were nearly numb by the repeated pressure. Lightly, almost distractedly, she massaged each of my legs as I lay on the cot. Vaguely I sensed her words and strokings surrounding me and wrapping me into a protected package. I was transported from the usual world of feelings and worries to a place of no sensation, no comprehension, where things would happen but not directly to me. I continued to hear her speaking and I knew she never took her hands from my body, but I could not then participate in what happened in the room. I had lain on the cot listening and floating for perhaps an hour when I was aware of a pressure, something pressing on my abdomen. I couldn't tell if what I felt was the doctor's hands kneading my diaphragm down, down, pushing, kneading, or whether something inside was pulling and sliding. In dreams I would be able to recapture the feeling, but never awake. In dreams I could hear moans and screams that I do not remember as my own. The hands on my stomach continued to stroke and press and soon I was able to focus better on what the doctor was saying.

"You see things differently out here in the countryside. Things that preoccupy you are not even contemplated by city folk. When they began advocating that city children spend time helping in the countryside, for the harvest or whatever, there was not even a murmur in the cities, until the children actually returned with tales of such a ridiculous life. 'Imagine,' they told us, 'no running water.' 'We had to take care of stupid, dirty animals and there were no proper baths to be had at all.' 'We ate very strange food and we had to do a lot of kitchen work, like peeling tomatoes and preparing beans. And this was apart from the work in the fields, manual, backbreaking work fit for mules.' There was no question of these children finding simplicity charming, seeing nature as it is and valuing it. The children in the cities are spoiled and will never adjust to life on farms. They will always be grudging about helping the poor farmers, doing foolish work for a few weeks because they are forced to do it. Even though Mary has led only a simple life in the city, a life without extreme luxury and comfort, but with more than the minimum, she will find life here on a farm as alien to her. But that is not Mary's main problem. She needs love. It will be her whole life before she is convinced that she will be loved. What Mary has been through is more than a revolution. Mary has lost her relationship with the past and the future; she can experience only the present and because it suits her, she avoids experiencing the present at all. She merely exists alongside us. Mary is like a war casualty, a battle-scarred veteran who has benumbed herself to the things around her she cannot absorb without pain. It is easier for her. Don't expect much from Mary; she has nothing much to offer and cannot accept much from you either. Life has been particularly cruel to Mary and the other children here in the convent, but it has not seen fit to ease their suffering with death."

Now she was helping me off the cot. She arranged some rags between my legs, made me take a few steps back and forth across the room, never leaving my side and never ceasing to talk her rhythmic words. She supported me as we walked from wall to wall of the small room and when to my own surprise I was able to walk independently, she helped me get dressed in the clothes I had been wearing.

"You are very strong, dear Egg Woman. You have done a courageous deed for which you will receive no medal. You and I will be the only ones who know what you deserve. I congratulate you for your compassion and sensitivity."

As I walked home slowly my head was spinning with notions and humming. I had little time in the weeks and months ahead to reflect upon that afternoon; how long it had been in all I never could reckon.

ELEVEN

Mary added to my responsibilities and didn't lighten my workload at all. She accompanied me everywhere, both because I couldn't trust her to do anything alone and because I liked to know where she was. She wasn't particularly cheerful to have around either. She was small and delicate and didn't like to dirty herself around the farm. Even without words, she complained about everything, which put all of us in a rather sour humor. I had to defend her against the children's argument that Mary should be sent away because she never did anything. I felt the same inclination to protest that she was needing more care than she returned in work. It was a new experience to have someone on the farm who actually did nothing, neither for herself, nor for the animals, nor for anyone else.

I can look back now and see the farm as perhaps Nathanael and Mary saw it. The animal droppings that covered the barnyard; droppings, and tufts of grasses struggling to emerge but discouraged by being immediately pruned by a chicken or cow or trod on by a hoof or foot. The smell was noticeable when you returned from an hour or two in the village. It was sweetish and full, it was the farm itself; at least, without the smell it would not be a farm at all. But for us the smell, the combination of manures from the pigs, the cows, the chickens, was our comfort, our familiarity. No other farm smells just the way ours does, each has its own perfume, like a house that takes on the smell of days of cooking and the odor of the wood used in the stove and the boots drying by the door and the bread baking and the soup on the stove. We sidestepped the piles with ease, knowing the favorite spots of the cow and the pigs. When we had it to spare, we would lay straw over the most obvious places, but usually we were accustomed to avoiding the piles without thinking. We were used to wearing barnyard boots and changing them when we came inside. When the boots were worn out beyond repair and we were in those days unable to replace them because they were made out of rubber and rubber had been rationed, we used our least-good shoes and left them at the door, wearing slippers in the house.

Mary was not used to droppings or anything else on the farm. She stepped unfailingly in the most obvious piles. Once when she had slipped and fallen she didn't say anything, didn't cry, didn't complain, but just as we were about to sit down to our meal, we had to interrupt and give Mary an extra bath and help her change her clothes. None of us could figure Mary out. The children criticized her endlessly; for them she did nothing right. They were not happy with my explanation that she was from the convent. They always treated things I said about anything but the farm as without merit. They couldn't believe I knew anything about even the village, much less anything on a larger scale. If I mentioned something about a subject they were learning in school or in the Youth, they would snort and tell me I knew nothing about it. Mary wasn't a member of the Youth, Mary didn't go to school, Mary was suspect, especially coming from the convent. There was something suspect in Mary's ignorance about the farm even.

It was quite true that Mary was no help to us at all.

Mary took to accompanying me on my trips into the village on market days. She carried some of the eggs gracelessly and wouldn't touch the chickens in any way. When it was time for me to make the delivery at the convent, Mary always stayed in the market square and waited for me there. One such occasion when I returned to the square I found several women standing around my stall with Mary in the middle. They were trying to decide among them where she came from. Mary herself said nothing, as usual, but the women in their gossipy way were speculating aloud about how I found her, where they thought they had seen her before, whether or not she was my daughter and so forth. My return surprised them, but their boldness was a vice they forgave themselves for its purity of purpose. They excused their prying and gossiping in the name of things of higher importance. I collected all the empty bundles and prepared to be on my way. I tried to ignore the women, but they had given themselves no limits.

"We were just wondering, dear Egg Woman, who this pretty little creature might be. Where did you find such a helpful little miss?"

They could see perfectly well that Mary was of absolutely no use whatever. I could hardly defend her on that score. So I just excused myself and told them I was in a hurry to be off home.

I asked Mary on the way home what these foolish women had been asking about, but she preferred not to discuss it with me. Actually Mary still refused to talk altogether. She didn't answer us and never asked for anything. She never defended herself if we yelled at her for doing something stupid or wrong, she just looked and made it impossible to continue chastising her. She was so indifferent to our scolding and attempts to teach her how to do something properly that we could see the uselessness of it all. The children were never reconciled to Mary's presence. They never imagined that she was nearly their own age. I felt tender toward Mary; there was something delicate about her that made me feel protective toward her. Her extreme remoteness alienated, as it was intended to do, the children, but made me even more patient and accepting of her.

Sister had hinted to me that the convent expected to be raided any day because someone had told the Gestapo about the children. The idea of the little children going to punishment camps after believing themselves to have found a safe haven in the convent was tragic, compounded by the plight of the sisters paying for having sheltered them. Although I knew I could be penalized for hiding Nathanael and I felt I could withstand the consequences, the shame and imprisonment, I was not comfortable that such a blot should stain the lives of my children, even though I did not think they would reciprocate the sentiment towards me.

The routine Nathanael and I had established seemed able to continue permanently. Mary's arrival altered that, seeming to multiply the chances of Nathanael being discovered. If Mary were challenged, it would jeopardize Nathanael's safety and my ability to protect him. I wondered how gladly I would accept punishment for defending Mary, knowing she had created the suspicion that would make Nathanael vulnerable.

At all times in the back of my thoughts were the things the doctor had spoken about. I dreamed frequently and sometimes I would wake up in a sweat, throat sore, to find Mary patting my arm gently, soothing my dream away. I would thank her and wonder what I might have said in my sleep that she may have understood. She was sensitive, one thought, though she herself said nothing.

I had continued to enjoy pleasures with Nathanael. He never lost his gentleness and genuine delight in my own delight. Nevertheless, the awareness that things would not always be as they were for us was beginning to grow. The arrival of Mary and my enlightenment about the activities in the convent and a partial comprehension of what things were like in the city and the pain that evidently had existed for years without my knowing about it, were asserting a place in my thoughts. As if dropped by some bird passing overhead, the idea that to live Nathanael would have to leave grew in my mind. I became distant. Slowly, yet by surprise, I realized it was over; my life would go on, but Nathanael would become a memory, a secret. Nathanael must have noticed a wistfulness or faraway look in my face, for he asked me about it.

"Have you found another lover, Eva?"

"Nathanael, what are you saying? How can you accuse me of such a thing?"

"I don't know, Eva, I must be losing my mind. Maybe I'm letting the chickens get to me. Who am I to be jealous of you?"

"That's not the point, Nathanael. How flattering to think that you might be jealous of me. But you can't expect me to be the same person you found when you first came to this chicken coop. Are you the same person you were? Not to me. You have changed from a stranger whom I had to teach how to string beans to a part of myself. You will never change back again into being a stranger. You will always remain what you are now for me, a part of myself, my life, me. I cannot seem to you the same person you first saw."

"It's true you have changed, as you say. First a complete stranger, a person one wouldn't stop to exchange words with on the street. Now intimate and known and special and loving and dear. But you are still innocent, simple, unaffected, direct and honest. Those things have not changed about you."

"So you say." I could not continue this line of conversation lest I be forced to explain where in fact I had changed and where not. I had known as soon as Karl described the trail he had marked in the mountains and his seeing Switzerland that he had shown me Nathanael's path to the future. At first I preferred to avoid thinking of it as something that would be needed any time soon, for that would mean that Nathanael would soon leave. How small-minded. How selfish. When I heard what the doctor had to tell me, I saw that there was no room for such egotism. Times had changed and selfish small motives had to give way to larger thoughts. This was bigger than sleeping together on a blanket in the chicken coop. Nathanael was not an isolated instance that had happened to only me. He was part of a greater event, not part of my life on this farm. Rather the farm was a small feature in a story written about the fortunes of many people I would never know. The doctor's stories had shown me some of what was going on outside the village, in the places where Nathanael and Mary had lived. I don't remember saying anything to the doctor that day—she hadn't expected conversation—she may not have realized the education she was offering me, but it was the first notion I had of how other lives are lived. While I recognized I did not know much about city life, I did not imagine how very different it could be from how we live on the farm.

I suffered from the lack of vision my life had allowed me. I had found life so predictable, the seasons, the weeks and days on the farm so similar from one year to the next. I had not known how different life was for others, their pain, their humiliation. Was I more worthy that I was entitled to things over others? Why should we enjoy privileges without deserving them? A decree might confer on me the right to own this farm, the right to go to school. Did I deserve it? And Nathanael not? And Mary? Would I find a decree declared that would force me to hide my children? Myself? Was there no limit to what might be?

TWELVE

One Friday at supper the children told me that it would be useless to take the extra eggs for the convent because they had heard that there were Jews in the convent and that they were to be arrested along with the sisters.

"What do you mean arrested? How can you arrest sisters?" I asked.

"You know, arrested. They take them away and they're arrested. Sisters are just like anybody else, or, well, you know, they can be arrested too if they hide Jews."

I decided to ignore Karl's warning and I presented myself at the convent as usual the next day. When I rang, Sister Karoline answered as usual, but she said she couldn't pay for the egg order.

"Take it anyway," I said. "You'll pay me some day. How are things with you?"

"Not good at all, Egg Woman," she replied. "We have lost some of our sisters. They have been arrested. They accuse us of treason because we refuse to sign the pledge of loyalty. We are going to lose the convent soon, because they claim we cannot own this property without signing the pledge. Even the few villagers we thought were friends are afraid to pass the time of day, much less come to pray in the church now. You may decide not to stop here as well. Perhaps it would be better for you."

"I'll be here next week, Sister Karoline. I have no fears."

That evening the children asked me about the convent and I told them that I had given them the eggs without payment. Karl became extremely agitated and struck the table with his hand. "Mamma, you are abetting traitors. Do you know what will happen to you? Do you know what the punishment is for abetting traitors? Do you know what will happen if they find out?"

"How will they find out that I let the convent have eggs on credit?"

"It's not as simple as that, Mamma. You sympathized with an enemy of the state. Do you know that Olga and I have sworn on our lives to protect the state? It is our duty to tell our superiors if there is anything threatening our security. Do you understand?"

"Karl, you can't think Sister Karoline is a threat to anyone? Or were you referring to me?"

"Mamma, you don't want to put Olga and myself in a compromising position. Do you know that my career might be in jeopardy if I know of a threat to the state and fail to inform my superiors about it? I might be forbidden entry into the special leadership school. This would be the end of my career before it could start. The group leader has told me he intends to recommend me to the school because of my dedication and trustworthiness. If he finds out I have known of treason and failed to report it, I will be left to tend chickens forever."

"You're not telling me that someone would consider that selling eggs to the convent is treason?"

"You know, Mamma, I am not the only member of the group who would like to attend leadership school. Anyone whose son is chosen for the school would be so proud. You would be beyond reproach as a mother to a leader candidate."

I looked up and the terror I saw in Mary's eyes silenced me. Was I now to begin debates with my children? Was there a question of state security in the identity of my customers? Mary and her terrible silence affected me and closed the discussion. I congratulated Karl on the honor he had achieved of being selected for leadership school.

I marveled at the ease with which I had taken to deception. Once begun, it was total; nothing remained untouched by my deception. Every moment of my day was planned around it and calculations of every movement were based on this deceit. The measurements for the stew, the laundry, what to carry to the chicken coop, when to collect the eggs. Everything I thought and did revolved around Nathanael's presence in my life. From his first frightened actions, there was never a moment when he was not in my thoughts and plans. I never hesitated. How would I know this would be for the rest of my life.

I cannot think of other deceptions before then. It had never been necessary. Even as a child I had never been a keeper of secrets. Once I learned the lesson of lying and I never had a taste for it after that. My father had asked me if I knew how the cow had gotten out of the barn. I did know, but I had found out only by accident. I had seen my sister forgetting to latch the barn door when she and the field hand went up to the hayloft and the wind had opened the door enough for the cow to drift out into the late afternoon sun. No great damage had been done, at least not as far as the cow was concerned. I found that I was tortured by the secret that I kept. I did not understand why the hot tears fell on my pillow, but when we sat at dinner the next evening and my father asked each of us in turn if we had left the door to the barn open so that the cow could get out I found the tears rising up to my eyes once more. I concentrated hard on my soup and kept the tears from falling and when my father asked me, I said no. Not actually a lie, but it felt like one to me. I have never been able to erase the feeling of conspiring with my sister that I felt. I wanted to go up to my father and confess, but I knew I would be confessing someone else's sins and I could not do it. I still felt the guilt crushing my chest with such strength that it affected my breathing. It seems an exaggerated reaction when I had done no wrong. Still, I was consumed with the subterfuge, the secret.

Deception had meant to hide something evil. I did not feel there was anything evil to hide. I didn't think of the present situation as deception at first. Initially, I had acted without deliberation. When I found out later what had brought Nathanael to the farm, I saw no reason not to continue.

Nathanael often thanked me for allowing him to stay. On the first anniversary of the day he had first appeared in the chicken coop he held me especially close and whispered so quietly in my neck that he was grateful to me. I was uncomfortable with the idea of Nathanael feeling indebted to me and I told him so.

"I owe my life to you, now and forever. Do you think I don't know it? Do you think I will forget it? How courageous you are every day. How strong you are. I often punish myself with the idea of leaving you to relieve you of me and the danger I bring. But I'm afraid. I want to live."

And I tell him to hush, that he doesn't have to worry about me or himself. That I too want him to live. As the days followed each other into the winter I became hard and sure. I began to plan and organize for Nathanael's departure.

Events and my own understanding led me to realize that the sooner Nathanael and Mary could be delivered to freedom the better their chances of survival would be. From what Karl had told me they should be on their way while the trees were in full leaf. Karl said that the views were better during the winter when the leaves had fallen. There were other risks in the spring because there would be more hikers on the paths. When I was sure that this was the only way to save them, that we could not be at all sure of continuing to keep them safe on the farm, I began preparations. After the lilacs faded in early May would be the earliest time, even though the leaves then would not be fully grown. I didn't talk to Nathanael about these plans, but I continued to think about what he would need.

In March there was news in the market that the army had taken over Austria. This was like a signal to me. After I heard this news in the village I went directly to the chicken coop to talk with Nathanael when Mary and I returned to the farm.

"Nathanael, I have heard some news in the village that concerns you."

"They speak about me in the village?"

"Not exactly, but they say the army has marched into Austria and taken it over."

"I suppose it was only a matter of time."

"Be that as it may, Nathanael, you are in danger here."

"And how do you figure that?"

"The villagers say that many people will be coming to our province to escape to Switzerland and even France. You must do so too, Nathanael."

"You want me to leave here?"

"You must leave here if you are to survive. I have understood that we are in a favorable position for you to arrive in Switzerland. They say don't go to France, only Switzerland, so that's where you must go."

"I see you've been thinking about this."

"Now we are preparing the fields. When harvest time comes, you have been a prisoner for nearly two years, including the camp. You have to make yourself strong, mentally and physically. We cannot allow these years to be lost, gone for nothing. We must win."

"I cannot believe you say such things. What's wrong with my staying right here? Does someone suspect? Have you heard gossip? Have you been plotting to get rid of me for all this time? I had nearly believed that there was something about this arrangement that halfway suited you. What has come over you? Do you not want to continue as we are?"

"Nathanael, we'll speak of this again, but now you must think about it. At first, I thought it was just you and me, but now I see we are only two of many. I didn't imagine this had anything to do with me. Then you came and I thought it was just for my pleasure that you were here. Now I realize that if they're hunting you I can't sleep. I am also hunted.

"I asked myself what about you was different and I do not yet know the answer. I thought politics was a faraway thing, but I found it living in my chicken coop. And the convent. It has taken me these many months to find that I am qualified to decide. I thought I was too stupid. I had never before met a Jew. I know now, even though I have never met a Chinaman, who he is. I thought this was complicated, but I discover even I, without schooling, a farm wife, an egg woman, can grasp the truth. When you hold me, Nathanael, you are a Chinaman too and I love you."

"Please leave me, Eva."

Nathanael was overcome with my words and I knew he didn't want me to see him cry.

I wasn't prepared for Nathanael's reaction when I broached the subject of escape that I had been thinking about for so long. I had made the decision without consulting him and it came to him as a surprise.

There was a sense that it would be easier to continue with Nathanael living in the chicken coop. We had become comfortable in our routine and it was working well. The adaptation Nathanael had made in the chicken coop had succeeded. We had found time for some enhancements, a bath at least once a month, often more than that, good meals, affection. Occasionally I brought a newspaper for Nathanael from town, pretending to wrap some greens in it. Rarely was there anything reliable in the paper, but Nathanael liked to read it and he read it over and over until I brought him another one. When the woman in the market bothered me about joining her group and subscribing to the monthly journal, I refused until I thought how much Nathanael might enjoy reading even this rubbish and I surprised him on his birthday with the first issue. He claimed he did enjoy it, but I think it wasn't so much for the cleverness of the journal as the respite it gave him from the official newspaper and another means of evaluating what might be happening elsewhere in the world. He never took any of it at face value, in fact he taught me to read the newspaper by contrariness—whatever the article stated was only possibly true in the opposite, possibly not even that but a half-truth. When they recommended using less fats in cooking for health benefits, actually they meant that because of the fat shortage there would be no butter or margarine available for cakes and other such items, so we had better find something as a substitute or forget about it altogether.

In any event Nathanael had made himself at home in the chicken coop. He had taken over the breeding of the chickens almost entirely. He gathered the eggs much of the time and watched the chickens. There were no sick chickens or chicken fights while Nathanael was living in the coop. He often singled out chickens that had begun to molt, often long before I would have noticed. He gently prodded chickens from the nests at night so that they would not get the broody habit and go out of production. After I explained to him what to watch for, Nathanael became an expert in advising me which birds I could count on and which should be culled, even though he detested the thought.

THIRTEEN

On a regular basis we had to contend with the visits of the Farm Bureau supervisor. Although he was not experienced with egg production, he used the guidelines from the central bureau to find certain defects and shortcomings in our operations. He criticized our method of mixing feed, about which he was correct, but we could not do otherwise. He wanted us to build a special room to keep only for the feed because we were unable to prevent certain infestations of bugs, and rats generally had access to the feed before we could finish with our supply. We could not construct such a separate room for feed, we needed our funds for other necessities before that. I would have had to hire someone to do the construction, in addition to the expense it would have necessitated for materials and so on. We always made it a practice to agree with whatever the Bureau man said. This was the policy that my husband had always followed and I saw the wisdom of continuing it. I prevailed on Karl to build a gangplank alongside the coop to one of the windows, so that the cat could catch any field mice that got inside.

We had enough distraction on the farm in the form of the cows, the vegetable garden, the pigs, that I was able to pass the time with the supervisor in discussions about everything but a visit to the chicken coop. On one occasion he expressed an interest in examining the coop and I naturally agreed that it would be a good idea and that in fact I had hoped he would have some suggestions for me in repairing or improving the coop so as to increase our egg output, but when the moment came as I had my hand on the latch to open the door, I quite offhandedly asked the supervisor if he had brought other shoes for I feared him tracking foreign organisms into the coop. Since he had nothing else to wear and rejected my offer of fetching a pair of my husband's boots, he never actually went inside the coop. I had an additional seven or eight arguments in readiness should he have gotten one or two steps closer, but that was never necessary.

We handled the farm supervisor well, in fact. I think we were one of his main sources for eggs, and he never looked too carefully at much of what went on on the farm. He more or less approved of Mary's joining us, remarking that we certainly could use the extra help.

In preparation for the Farm Bureau man's visit, usually at monthly intervals, though it could vary, we would spruce up certain areas of the farm that we generally ignored because we considered them less important for the running of the farm. It was clear that the Farm Bureau man could choose any number of ways that the farm failed to maintain proper standards: either he could criticize sanitation in the feed room, complain that we didn't recycle the manure more carefully, or find bugs in the water trough. Animals had taken to living in the hay stall because we failed to stir up the hay regularly. Rats often shared the feed because we sometimes left it uncovered or forgot to fill up holes under the door. On this particular day, in late August 1938, the sun high and hot, with the undertone of coolness the evening would bring, I went to check the chicken cage where we isolated birds for sale. I found one that Nathanael had noticed and selected out for some puffiness around her eyes and discoloration on her beak. She was doing poorly and showed signs now of more advanced disease. In view of the impending visit of the Farm Bureau man in the next few days, I took hold of this hen and prepared to do away with it. For cooking I usually used a knife to kill a bird, but this time, not wanting the blood to contaminate anything in case the bird was contagious, I just yanked its neck, one quick pull. I took the bird into the house where I had started a kettle of water boiling and dunked the bird in upside down, holding its legs. I said the alphabet one time slowly and lifted it out and pulled off the feathers. Then I went over to the burn barrel where we incinerated our garbage. I put the bird in, sprayed it with kerosene and lit the fire. Mary had been trailing behind me during these maneuvers, really the first time she had seen me weeding the birds. When she saw that I was burning the bird she began crying quietly.

"Mary, dear, don't be alarmed. The bird was sick and might have infected the others and that would have been a disaster. The Farm Bureau man will be here soon and if he saw that bird he might have condemned our entire farm. He might have told me all my eggs would have to be destroyed. He might not let me sell any more. That would be the end of us all. Don't cry, Mary, we have other chickens."

But Mary couldn't be consoled. She was horrified and stood shaking as the chicken burst into flames and popped and sputtered in the fire. She had never thought of the animals as anything but pets. She was sensitive to their treatment from her city perspective, refusing to connect the food on her plate to the animals in the barnyard. The smell of the burning chicken, usually so appetizing, this time was mixed with the aroma of the fuel and whatever garbage had remained in the barrel and it pervaded the entire farm. As I approached her, Mary shrank from my touch as though I, capable of this outrage, might be capable of any other.

I was often reminded of how unsuited Mary was to farm life. It was ridiculous to contemplate her remaining long on the farm, eventually she would give herself away. That was no doubt why she had been first on the list to leave the convent. Karl and Olga were never completely reconciled to having Mary on the farm. She, for so long completely silent, now seemed to be opening herself up to what she could of farm life, but her nature was opposed.

It can't be said that Mary became part of our family. We were far from being what others might construe as a family even before Mary came to the farm. While joined by blood, we otherwise were united in little else. Each placed his or her own needs before anyone else's and before the farm's; each concentrated on his or her projects, only providing for the generality when there was spare time. During the period when I was in charge, I required of Olga and Karl very little. After Nathanael came, I actually preferred it when they left me alone. Though I was quite in control of my behavior, in fact I was more relaxed than before, I still preferred not to have them on the farm. I had little to worry about; they too preferred to spend their time with their groups, in their room or on special Youth trips and studies.

Mary remained peculiar. She sometimes answered me. That is, if I insisted, just to be reassured that she had a working voice, she would answer me out loud rather than just shaking her head or nodding her answers. She spoke to no one else. The animals even shied away from Mary, as if they sensed her strangeness. She was unable to follow any instruction, she could not be relied upon for anything at all, even her own care. I responded to her silence and remoteness by refusing to acknowledge them as peculiar. When she didn't answer something, I never showed anger or irritation, I accepted her totally as one accepts a cow's silence and refusal to answer. Mary was adjusting to being with me and I could tell in a few ways that she accepted me and understood that I was not an enemy. Her silence threatened me because it was clear she was intelligent and merely chose to close us off from her. I worried that she might discover the fact that Nathanael was hiding in the chicken coop: she might notice the extra food, which was now double extra because of her; she might in some way figure out that something was not normal. She was always present. I could not get rid of her, to the far pasture, or the vegetable patch, or anywhere. She was an obstacle for Nathanael, in that he could no longer take his baths in the house; he never again spent the night in my bed. Nathanael, of course, never complained about these or any other things. I thought of the bath and brought him extra water and soap so he could wash in the coop. He understood what it meant, but never made reference to why we now had to resort to this system. Since Mary never asked questions, I had no way of knowing what, in fact, she might have noticed, so I suspected her of noticing everything and was more cautious than ever. When I had a scrap of newspaper to show Nathanael, neither of the children would have commented at its presence or absence on the corner of the table, but I wondered if perhaps Mary had seen it there and then noticed its unexplained absence. She would never say, of course. In this way Mary provided a negative factor on the farm. The Farm Bureau representative saw Mary as a contributor to the work of the farm and expected us to increase both egg production and the size of the flock. He calculated the farm workers as four, indicating that he would expect a certain output from a farm the size of ours with four people working it. We never came close, since he should have calculated based on a bit more than one person running the farm, only me. With the focus narrowing more and more to only the chickens and the eggs, I had more reason to spend time in the chicken coop. Anything I could do to improve either the coop structure or the feed or the conditions of the flock was positive. So the more time I spent in the coop or around the chickens appeared to be work time. It was far from true. The longer Nathanael stayed the more things we found to talk about. Our relationship was becoming more complex with each day; our interdependency was deepening and our attachment was strengthening. I was the only human being Nathanael touched and spoke to all the time he spent on the farm. His dependence on me was obvious. I knew that I relied on him and had integrated him into my life.

My first thought each morning was of Nathanael. Immediately I gained consciousness with the roosters I looked forward eagerly to seeing Nathanael. There was the protective element to this anticipation and the intimate. I felt that if I ascertained that Nathanael was there and secure first thing in the morning, when I went to feed and water the chickens, the whole day would be safe, Nathanael would be safe. Also I was to a great degree calmed by our first brief but warm embrace of the day. Nathanael would enclose me slowly and strongly, standing with me among the growing cackle, he too perhaps relieved that I was still there to protect him. I would have felt myself a failure had

Nathanael been captured on the farm. That was why when we heard of the attack on the convent I felt an urgency for him to leave and find total safety.

"But what do you mean by total safety, Eva? What makes you think that will exist when I cross a border?"

"Nathanael, don't try for too sharp an edge with me. You know what I mean. The sisters knew so many things, in particular, Mary. How do we know at this moment Sister Karoline has not been forced into telling the Gestapo about Mary and where she is? Who is to say we are not being spied upon at this very moment?"

In truth I did not think Sister Karoline would ever reveal anything to the Gestapo, even under torture, but out of so many others and children at the convent, there was risk. This desire on my part to see Nathanael safe had to do with the notion of fulfilling my job successfully. Protecting Nathanael meant that he should survive, not for the months he lived in the chicken coop, but forever. Had I preserved Nathanael for my personal pleasure? Was he my secret plaything? It wasn't possible any longer to consider Nathanael simply from my own personal point of view. Whatever significance he had for me, in my life, was only subsidiary to his place in his own society. I didn't fool myself that he had come simply to give me the warmth and tenderness he had given me. I thought about the sisters in the convent being herded into vans, taken away from their home and lives, perhaps yelling, refusing, being pushed and manhandled to leave. They were seeing the people they had tried to protect thrown about along with them, and they must have been doubly tortured at the thought that they had failed to keep them safe. Despair and fear at one's own arrest and pain and guilt and worry at the others'. This was a scene I could not bear enacting here on the farm with myself and Nathanael as the players. I would not erase the beauty of the past nearly two years, the delicate relationship Nathanael and I had created, with an ugly ending. Better he should go immediately than spend an extra day for the Gestapo to find him. I didn't worry about being arrested. I had no reason to think how dire the consequences might be, unrealistically so. I imagined arrest and release, not torture and death. Nathanael, I knew, expected the worst for himself, quite rationally. He lived for those two years thinking I was sparing him certain death. I did not then know the truth of that. I suspected he was exaggerating, but I had no way of supporting my disbelief. The power of his feelings for me in part may have emerged from his conviction that my protection was saving him from death. I had never needed to argue this point, though I did not believe it.

In my bed, with Mary beside me, I lay awake listening to the silence and the space around the farm. With Nathanael in the coop, my need to assure his safety, to get him away, was intense and definite. The risks he might incur on the way seemed slight compared to those he ran of being discovered in my coop, unacceptable to me, and more unthinkable as it seemed more likely. I tried to approach the subject gently but being with Nathanael reminded me of what I would be losing. This second sacrifice, giving Nathanael up, was what would validate the first one, endangering myself in the first place. Somehow there was no way of looking at the situation and concluding otherwise.

Still there were things to be discussed. Convincing him to go. When? How? With Mary? I had to be sure he would follow my instructions exactly in order to be certain he wouldn't be caught. He had to trust me and I had to trust myself that I knew what to do. Taking Mary presented a handicap for him, but there was no real question in my mind about it. Mary had to go with him. Since I asked it, he had to comply. I would have to depend on the Nathanael I knew to protect Mary. I knew that if I asked it, Nathanael would adopt my desire that Mary would make it to safety as well. I pointed out to Nathanael that everything we had suffered for Mary would be in vain should she be discovered. She would never be able to defend herself, clearly, and he would be able to guide her to safety somewhere. The hindrance she would present had to be borne. Nathanael would understand.

"You want Mary to come with us?"

"Us?"

"Who then?"

I couldn't speak. This was something I had not considered at all. Nathanael thought I would be leaving with him? He had misunderstood me completely. He feared being on his own after these years of developing the habit of deferring to me for so many things. I was devastated by this supposition. The reality of our coming separation was too much for me, opening before me like a gorge that appears without warning. I stood up and left the chicken coop without another word and walked out beyond the vegetable patch, up the rise and over to the other side.

Before I could control my sobs I realized Mary had followed me as usual, probably as soon as she saw me leave the coop. I was beyond control at that point. Mary was shocked because she had never seen me so emotional, never seen me without total possession of myself. At first Mary was terrorized by the despair she read in my heaving body; she didn't know how to help me, whether I was ill or injured. Then for the first time since she had come to live with us Mary voluntarily spoke to me.

"My dear Egg Woman, you must be strong. We need you to be strong. What can I do for you? How can I help you? Please, Egg Woman, do not cry so."

My hysteria was not to be quelled even by the surprise of Mary's attempts to soothe me. I was discharging two years of anxiety and anguish. The sobs that shook my body were akin to the spasms of childbirth, a natural expulsion of what has matured and ripened. Mary put her arms around me and murmured in my neck and hair, trying to tell me that she was sorry, that she wanted to help me, that she loved me. She sat with me where I had collapsed on the grass. My breath was erratic from the sobbing, causing me to straighten up to gasp for air now and then, having exhaled too much. Finally, after some time, I regained my senses and dissolved into normal crying, sniffling and occasionally gasping for new breath like a child after a temper tantrum. After a few more minutes, I wiped my face with my apron and blew my nose with my handkerchief and sat back on my heels and took a look at Mary, still with an arm around my shoulder. Her face told me she knew the despair I felt, that there was no cure for it, that to be alive is to despair. She did not comfort me with hope, with denial, with argument. She shared the emptiness and sadness I felt.

Mary might one day face her life as I was doing that day and see how futile it is to struggle against what one is. Without understanding much of the forces that had contributed to make me the person I was, I knew that it made no difference. Even if I could chronicle the generations that had gone before and influenced my being just here on a knoll behind this particular farmhouse, I could not change it. Believing one or another way was the better, disbelieving or believing in nothing had no bearing on Nathanael in the chicken coop. My life was to be a farm woman. I had nothing without it. I could not conceive of reversing places with Nathanael, of being hunted, threatened, displaced. That would not be me. I was limited by being a farm woman. Otherwise I was nothing. I was either the farm woman who had taken Nathanael into the chicken coop or I didn't exist at all. I could not become someone else. All along I had known, within my heart, that this was not forever. I had to live through this ending. Probably Nathanael similarly could not accept the logic of someone willingly remaining amidst such unsavory circumstances. Voluntarily. There was no logic to it, but it was inevitable. Even our closeness could not reduce the pull of generations within me.

I now put my arm around Mary and we sat there on the grass hugging one another in mutual sorrow, each aware that changes had taken place between us, and within us. As we walked back to the house I realized that it would not be long before she would be privy to the secret in the chicken coop.

The change in Mary was immediately noticeable to everyone. Nathanael heard Mary's voice and commented at how now she even spoke to the animals, as we always had done. Karl and Olga exchanged glances when they heard Mary ask for a piece of bread at dinner. They didn't dare make any remarks, but in a household with little chatter and useless gossip, Mary's occasional contributions could not be ignored. Mary was still quiet and reluctant with Olga and Karl and never spoke to them unnecessarily. With me, when we were alone, she always reached for my hand to hold or part of my clothing to touch. She allowed her craving for affection, so long denied, to emerge for short instances, having broken down whatever had prevented it before. I understood little of Mary's thinking and accepted her as she was. I returned easily and gratefully her gestures of comfort, or so I interpreted her reaching out toward me. She was at last able to give to one who seemed to need her, at least at that moment, more than she needed anyone.

When I was again able to talk with Nathanael, I could not raise the subject with him. I felt despair rising to close my throat, a presence in my body that pressed on my chest and threatened me if I didn't change my thoughts. Nathanael, naturally, preferred not to discuss leaving, hoping that I had given up the idea altogether. Now I never stopped thinking about it, however, turning it around and trying new ways of approaching it. I practiced imaginary conversations with Nathanael, trying to get him to do what I wanted without specifying what that was. The idea of my joining Nathanael or Nathanael and Mary in leaving the country was beyond my capacity to imagine. I was the farm. I could not use the farm and then run from it as they could. I was not threatened when they were not there. I could continue to live as before, on the farm, doing farm work, raising the chickens, selling the eggs. That was me and my life. I had to preserve that. In some way there was a half thought that if I could send Nathanael and Mary off to safety, to life, I might do it again with others. It was implied, wasn't it, in my continuing on the farm? If they were successful in surviving, through the farm, others could survive too. I could think about Nathanael leaving if I could give what he had given me to others. Nathanael had shown me a need, shown me how I could fill that need, by maintaining the farm, keeping in the good graces of the Farm Bureau man, keeping the egg business going. In that way I could provide a service. Nathanael had shown me an evil and challenged me to do what I could to erase it, or some of it, at least. I found I could compensate for that evil by helping Nathanael to survive it. But what good would it do if I left with him?

Was it selfish of me to want to hold on to the feelings Nathanael stirred within me? Was Nathanael afraid it would be selfish of him to leave me behind among the evil, endangering myself with someone else while he was living safe and free?

After the raid on the convent, nothing continued as before. There was a hastening, a presence hovering, circling above the farm. The daily routine drew me along, pulling me from one chore to the next, forcing me into activity when in other times and places I might have chosen to spend the day in meditation or staring into space or under the bedcovers. I couldn't avoid seeing Nathanael every day, now tortured by his gentleness and delicacy. How I would have liked to remove the thought of Nathanael's leaving from between us, and within me. Nothing that happened gave me even a feather's weight of pause or reconsideration. Whether there was logic or not, Nathanael and Mary would leave together and I would stay behind.

Mary made a more comfortable companion for me after she began to speak. She continued to follow me throughout the day; now, instead of simply watching me, she sought to do what I did. She had still no idea of how to do most of the chores, but her cleverness seemed to increase with her congeniality. She soon was the principal water drawer, making countless trips from the well to the water trough, to the kitchen and back again. Rather than pulling the full bucket's worth, Mary could carry only about half a bucket and so her chore was multiplied. I never noticed Mary growing at all, but she seemed to gain strength in the weeks that followed, as if she knew she would require it. When I gathered the clothes and sheets together for laundering, Mary joined me and copied my movements, anxious to learn and lighten the load she now perceived I was carrying.

Time isn't something one is terribly aware of on the farm. Days don't distinguish themselves, one from another; events are so small that one rarely remembers which precedes or succeeds another. The circle of life rolled around in time with the seasons, but on a daily basis barely perceptible. Still there was for me a feeling of push, of movement, of limits and deadlines. Karl and Olga came home one day and announced that they had been chosen by the Youth, as a brother-sister team, to attend the national rally in Nuremberg. The Youth would pay for the trip and their stay and they would be joining children from all over the country to march and celebrate the state together. Karl was overjoyed that he had been selected for higher leadership posts and he was ecstatic at the thought of seeing the leader in person and hearing his speech. Olga too was bright with the reflected glory of her brother that had included her in this special occasion.

Karl was anticipating attending his leadership school and when I saw him at his moving-up ceremony I hardly recognized him in his uniform and haircut. He was nearly eighteen and from a distance was indistinguishable from any one of his fellow Youth members. Olga, my girl, a year younger, was looking forward to her year of service in the city. She expressed some doubts about leaving me alone with Mary. It was part of that perverse time that the complications Olga and Karl created would disappear just when Nathanael and Mary would no longer be there to worry about.

As usual the national rally would be in September, a few weeks hence. This was my cue to complete the plans for Nathanael and Mary to leave. Here was a ready-made deadline. With the children gone, I thought, I would be able to use the camping gear that they would leave behind.

Karl would not take with him the compass, the canteen, eating implements, the rucksack. Timing their departure to coincide with the rally was quite propitious since so many people would have their attention glued on the events around the rally. Anyone thinking of a vacation just then would likely go north toward Nuremberg, rather than the Black Forest. I would get everything ready and only tell them perhaps one day before, maybe not until the day itself.

As the end of summer neared, Karl and Olga, preparing full-time for their exciting journey, their first of any distance, concentrated only on their uniforms and their physical conditioning. They would be attending meetings and workshops and learning new things, as well as practicing for the big rally. They were so proud, really, one could hardly think of puncturing their complacent self-satisfaction. Often in those days they remarked how proud their father would be of them and their dedication and discipline. Over the years I had watched these Youth tasks take priority over their school lessons. One could do nothing.

Finally they left. I hadn't seen them smile so continuously since they were babies. The night that they left I told Mary she could sleep in one of their beds, but she said she preferred to sleep with me. We had become used to each other. As we lay together, I realized that I had taken Mary quite for granted in this scheme. I had continued to think of her as a silent child when in reality she now was a quiet, small adult. Since there were barely two days before I had planned for them to leave, I had to prepare Mary for another change in her life, one she would look forward to even less than Nathanael.

"Mary, can you hear me?"

"Yes, Egg Woman."

"We must talk, my Mary, we must talk."

"What about?"

"It's time for you to leave, Mary."

"I'm never leaving you, Egg Woman. You've saved me, you're good to me, you're my family. Have I displeased you?"

"No, Mary. This is for your own sake. You must save yourself."

"I'm safe here with you."

"No, Mary. It seems like safe now, but this will not, cannot last. Things are not going well. You know they have taken away the sisters and want to close the convent. All the other children who were staying with the sisters have been taken away. They'll come for you too one day, and I will not be able to save you any more than the sisters could save those other children."

"In that case, I'll take my chance with you. The sisters were not so kind to me, you know. They greeted me coldly, they didn't really want me there and they got rid of me as soon as they could. I admit I wasn't the favorite of the sisters, because it wasn't my way to cuddle. We both know perfectly well I am not 'Mary.' I am Rebecca and I am Jewish. That's why all this is happening to me. I know what happened to my father and his store and all the people we knew. We are not wanted. But you want me, don't you, Egg Woman?"

"Mary...shall we continue with 'Mary' or would you prefer 'Rebecca'?"

"Perhaps we should continue with 'Mary,' even though I know who I am and what my name is."

"It'll be easier to continue then with 'Mary.' Mary, I want you. But it cannot be. This isn't going to be easy to explain, but I'll have to trust that you will understand that nothing is easy these days."

"Egg Woman, I have found myself finally at peace here with you. You're not going to get rid of me now. I know that one day they'll come and drag me off and take me to some disgusting place. Until that day I will be with you."

"No, Mary, that is not how it will be. You may not want to listen to reason, but one day, of this I am absolutely sure, you will tell yourself that I was right. Until then I will ask you to obey, particularly since it is not you alone involved." My voice had taken on authority from some unknown source. I spoke to Mary as if this had always been what was planned, only she had not been told. "What will happen is that you and Nathanael will walk to freedom across the border. You will again be among strangers, but Nathanael will take care of you. Everything will be strange, but you will never be dragged off by police and taken to any disgusting place. You will never be threatened. You will be free to decide yourself what to do. Your father and mother hope that you will quickly pull yourself together, see that the future was given to you by them, and educate yourself, have a beautiful family, live a long life and be as happy as possible. You will always remember your mother and father, you will never forget Sister Karoline, gruff and cold though she was, you will never forget me, the egg woman who learned to know you and love you." I put my arms around Mary and held her close to me, letting my tears fall on her shoulders, patting her back gently, knowing I would never forget her. I would never ever comprehend the forces that caused Mary's life to bend and twist as it did, but I knew the role I had to play in it was to end.

"Mary, listen to me carefully. You must control your emotions as I must mine. Do not doubt that what must be done is according to your parents' wishes. Let's go now and meet Nathanael. It's time."

We covered our nightdresses and slipped on some shoes and went out into the cool September air, where the moon shone with the faintest glow. As we approached the chicken coop, Mary stopped and looked at me with her mouth agape. She obviously had no clue whatever that a person might be there. I held her around her shoulders and pressed her close to me, letting her know I had not lost my senses.

As soon as I touched the door of the chicken coop, I spoke out. "Nathanael, Mary and I have come to see you tonight. We have been talking about you and the journey you and Mary will make."

I heard the board being removed from the hiding place in the floor where Nathanael had taken refuge as soon as he heard Mary's and my footsteps approaching. In a moment we could see Nathanael's shadow emerging from under the roost, where his secret place was.

Mary gasped with eyes widened as Nathanael emerged into the dimly lit part of the coop. His beard and hair now were nicely trimmed, his clothes clean. His tall frame was lean, though not more so than others in our area. The only slightly comical touch were Nathanael's spectacles, which still had one lens cracked and an ear-piece askew, but which he refused to do without. She took a step closer to me and seeing in my face no alarm whatever she relaxed a bit.

"Good evening, Mary," said Nathanael, extending his hand toward Mary. "Welcome to my house. Please come in and stay awhile. It will be so nice to have someone to chat with. I wish I could offer you something to eat, but at the moment we have only some chicken feed about."

Nathanael's attempt at calming Mary was far from a success. It was also so out of character for him that it struck me as offensive as well, that tone of sarcasm and mock-apology.

"Nathanael, please, Mary and I have been discussing her leaving and I realized that it was time for the two of you to meet. Mary, you understand that it would have been impossible for you to have met Nathanael before this. He has been living in this chicken coop for nearly two years now. He was a university student and was arrested because he is Jewish. He escaped from a camp and took refuge in this chicken coop. You and he will make the journey across the border together."

"Eva, you speak as if it were already decided," said Nathanael.

"It is," I said in my newly found voice of authority. With both of them together, I found I could easily maintain this unemotional distant attitude. I could not permit any dissension on this question. "You and Mary will set out for the Black Forest and in two nights of walking will cross the border and begin new lives of freedom."

"You have decided."

"Not only I have decided, but we have all agreed on it. We all know what we want for each other. We know what we want for ourselves. We all know about sacrifice and hardship and hunger. Now you and Mary will find out about freedom. That is what I want. I want you and Mary to have a life without having to depend on my protection. I'm not enough. Who would say the sisters could not protect the children living there? Who would swear this farm will always find the protection of the Farm Bureau man? I am only one. You must find a place where you don't need the protection of one egg woman to stay alive. This cannot be."

I began to cry softly. I had wanted to scream those words, but something about the presence of the chickens and being in the chicken coop restrained me out of habit. But the earnestness with which I spoke was plain enough. Nathanael looked at Mary and they both came to comfort me. Their own courage, which had been unnecessary as long as mine had been on watch, now asserted itself. Nathanael acknowledged silently that I was right; Mary would only acquiesce reluctantly, still too immature to evaluate her own needs.

Nathanael, his arm still around me, said, "You will come with us?"

"No, Nathanael, I will not. You and Mary will think of me here on the farm, coming every day to the chicken coop. I will think of you walking about under cover of the dark trees, walking to a place where you can live without fear. Nathanael, you will take care of Mary, I know, until she is settled and safe. You will please continue your studies and have a family and live a long life. I will be happy knowing this will happen."

Nathanael had conceded. Perhaps he had been thinking about it and acknowledged that this would be best. Mary reverted immediately to the safety of her earlier silence, a cushion to this new rejection and an instant fear of further attachment to me. I accepted her silence gently and without rancor. She was right.

Nathanael and I had no further moments alone.

The next day the three of us spent in the house going over the provisions I had gotten from Karl's camping gear. I taught Mary and Nathanael how to use the compass and described the trail Karl and his mates had blazed through the forest. I knew that even if they failed to find it, they would still get to the border if they followed the compass. Now they were both eager to be off and I was urging them to wait for sundown. They had to accede to this last request of mine and we watched the sun disappear, leaving its last light.

Nathanael and Mary had in a few hours cemented a partnership. Nathanael's customary gentleness and his acceptance of the soundness of their leaving on this journey had squelched any objections Mary might still have harbored.

During the day there were constant references to Mary and you or Nathanael and you, so that it seemed hardly possible that Mary had not known of Nathanael's existence only one day earlier. Nathanael was clever though not overly practical and Mary was compliant though hardly adventuresome. It seemed more likely than not that they would succeed. I was sure of it and told them so more than once, hoping to stifle any doubts either one might have had.

When they left, Nathanael holding me so long until I could not bear it and pulled away, Mary, her arms about my neck and her little body trembling and shaking with sobs, I was bereft.

Some weeks later a postcard arrived with a Swiss postage stamp and postmark, addressed to the Egg Woman, in care of the convent, with two signatures: "Chicken Man" and "Rebecca."

In proud memory of my grandparents

David Davis
born Jedwabne, Russia (now Poland), 1873
died Brooklyn, New York, 1961

Dora Innerfield Davis
born Myszyniec, Russia (now Poland), 1883
died Long Beach, New York, 1969

Abraham Hyman
born Plonsk, Russia (now Poland), 1869
died New York, New York, 1920

Rose Weiss Hyman
born Plonsk, Russia (now Poland), 1879
died New York, New York, 1973

Brave adventurers in the new world,
so we were spared the fate of those who remained behind.